ISBN 90-225-3192-9

TOM'S ADVENTURES AT SEA

The story and Adventures of Tom A Boatman from Deal

By David Skardon

Shaking out herring on Deal Beach
Fishing boat." Spray."
Circa 1970

This book is dedicated to all the boatmen that worked and plied from Deal beach, their valor and unseen services to their fellow man can only be appreciated by those that were helped, and the reward from our creator above.

Although a thing of natural beauty, the sea is respected and not taken for granted by all of us boatmen and fishermen that sail on her.

I would also like to thank David Lawrence for contributing the picture of Sprat landings.

FOREWARD

A story based on the real working lives of the Boatmen of Deal, Kent, a small fishing town on the South East coat of England.
Deal is protected by a large sandbank some 6 miles wide and 15 miles long, its closest point is 2 miles off shore, this stretch of sand is known as the shippe swallower, or the ."Goodwin Sands." it is also surrounded by many other treacherous sandbanks, which over time have all, taken their toll of shipping.

For hundreds of years ships of all kinds have taken shelter in the downs off Deal, many hundreds have been lost to the notorious Goodwin Sand

Boats have always been launched from the shingle beach at Deal, and Boatmen were known as the most skilled seamen on the English coast, giving aid and rescue to stricken vessels, running pilots, smuggling and fishing, whatever the following the work was hard and poorly paid.

This story is about Tom, a young lad growing up on the beach, his father is a boat owner and fishmonger. We follow him on some of his exploits from the Herring fishery, once a large thriving industry during the months of October to January, to his adventures in saving ships and cargoes from the Goodwin Sands.

Sadly all the boats except a couple, and the men that were so skilled in operating them have now gone, due to modern rules and regulations, causing the demise of the boats on the fore shore.

The story is set in the late 1890's to the early 1900's, and follows Tom, an up and coming Boatman on Deal beach, we join him hauling off to catch some herring. Then following him on some of his adventures and rescues around the Goodwin Sands in the boats that are worked from Deal beach, and the hazards he encountered.

CONTENTS

Page No:

Chapter 1	The Launch	page	7
Chapter 2	The Drift	page	14
Chapter 3	Ashore at Last	page	32
Chapter 4	The Night Haul	page	51
Chapter 5	The Wreck of the Frederick	page	69
Chapter 6	A Good Days Work	page	86
Chapter 7	Behind the Goodwins	page	106
Chapter 8	The Trip to Lowestoft	page	131
Chapter 9	The North Sea Fishing Grounds	page	142
Chapter 10	Homeward Bound	page	181
Chapter 11	The return to Lowestoft	page	192

Illustrations

Front page   Shaking out herring on Deal Beach, the Motor boat." Spray." circa 1970

Page 141   A Lugger under full sail

Page 191   A Good catch of Sprats

CHAPTER ONE

THE LAUNCH

It had been a long dreary week of storm force winds from the sou-west, reaching hurricane force twelve on several occasions. The downs were crowded with ships of all nations and types, seeking shelter from the heavy seas which had been raging over the last few days; mountainous pillars of water could be seen rising up on the horizon, as tons of water was thrown in violence upon the treacherous Goodwin Sands; the place of death for many a fine seagoing vessel.

It was early November, the herring season had been in full swing for a few weeks, but catches were very poor, the winds had been constantly blowing from the sou-east, making fishing difficult, and thus clearing the water to a degree where one would be mistaken, if it were not so cold, for looking into the blue Mediterranean Sea.

A welcome relief came on the ninth day of the storms, which had, during their course and violence, suddenly abated. Ships in the downs weighed anchor,*setting out once more into the open North Sea, on their journeys, filled with all sorts of cargoes.

The sea for some hours off Deal was splendor of sail and steam, each and every vessel slowly taking their place in line to pass through the Gull Stream and out to the northern end of the Goodwins, to the safety of the open sea.

Considerable damage had been done along the water front, with the beach being washed over the sea wall and carried far down the side streets to the town centre, giving the effect of a town built more on shingle, than the quaint little place it previously resembled, with the clean narrow streets lined with smart painted fisherman's houses, only broken in places by the occasional shop and public house. Winches had been eroded from their mooring places, and were dragged by the huge swells almost to the low waters edge, large chunks of the promenade were lifted from their fixings and thrown into the streets; leaving gaping holes and cavities in the once smooth and flat walkway which on a calm sunny day would be crowded with visitors; houses on the sea front had their windows broken by the shingle that was thrown upon them by the heavy pounding swells.

Boats all along the fore-shore had been washed into side streets and many were damaged; boat woods, old drums, seats, nets, in fact almost everything had been removed from its berth and washed into the town, there were even a couple of paddle punts in the high street, carried down Broad Street by the huge seas, these had now been put to better use and were ferrying people to and fro the flooded shops, a storm of such magnitude and violence had not been recorded on these shores for many hundreds of years.

The tide had ebbed away and the wind was almost at a dead calm, with clear blue skies striking from behind the last of the clouds, which were clearing from the west'ard, although a heavy swell still persisted in covering the beach in glistening white foam.

Taking an account of the situation on the beach, the task of putting right the damage commenced. The boat was manually and painstakingly heaved back across the road, once again to sit upon its greased boards proud and ready to launch. Tons of beach had to be shoveled seaward, clearing a way for the boat to gain access to the water, which was her workplace, as this was one of the few remaining commercial fishing boats left on Deal beach, not having the pleasure of the easy life of the angling charter boats which some of the other boatmen had adopted for a living. Herring nets were withdrawn from her hold, cleared and re-stowed ready for the next tide.

Many hours of grueling work of preparation and clearing up saw the day pass quickly, thank God for the grace He now showed us, it had been a long time with no earnings, but the stir up was well needed, with luck, we would now see some good catches of herring, and once again be able to afford the small comforts of a piece of meat for dinner, and a pint of beer to wash it down.

Ready! At last, everything was ready and prepared for launching on the midnight tide, that's if the swell had subsided enough to make a launch possible. Time had allowed for a couple hours sleep, so curled up on the floor by a warm fire I slipped into the quiet land of peaceful dreams until eleven that night.

Awakened by the sound of loud bells, I jumped swiftly to my feet, not quite knowing where I was, or what was happening. It was the alarm, what a relief, I was stuck in the middle of a dream, from which these bells seemed to take a lifelike and realistic part. Slowly gaining access to my whereabouts it came to me what had occurred during the last twenty four hours, now awake and realizing that arrangements had been made to launch on the midnight tide. I quickly dressed and refreshed with a cup of hot tea then left the house and set about the task in hand.

The night was calm and clear, with a twinkling of frost upon the ground, which crunched below my feet with every step as I walked through the church yard towards the beach, the crashing of the swells could be heard right through the town, breaking the quietness of the night, it didn't sound too good, there was still a lot of sea running by the sounds of it. Steadily I made my way up to the beach, and came up to the plots where my boat lay, standing up pride fully in the moonlight on its stocks, almost glaring at me with envy, eager to be launched so she could show off on the glistening moonlit sea.

Standing along side her was the tall thin shadow of a middle aged man, dressed in thigh boots and oilskin, caressing the horizon and watching the swells as they rose up and crashed onto the beach, still with ever increasing ferocity.

"Good evening mate." I said, as I came up to him," still a heavy swell running isn't there."

He turned his face towards me, showing the dark salt burnt lines of his years at sea in his cheeks, it was my skipper

"Aye Tom," he said,"It looks like we won't be going afloat tonight Tom, the seas running up the beach too high."

The sea certainly was running up the beach very high, and at present would make launching very difficult, although it was still about an hour till high water and normally at that period there would be a short time where the sea would become less ferocious, and a boat would be able to launch.

"Might die away a bit when the flood takes hold of her." I said to him." Are you going to wait until the top of the tide and see?"

Again he turned towards the sea looking out beyond the swell

"There's a calm every seventh swell." he exclaimed." But with just the two of us, it's going to be mighty difficult to launch into that there soft; if we get stuck we've had it you know."

The beach was what we call soft, as most of the shingle had been replaced by a very fine stone, which on contact acted more like quick sand, if the boat hesitated during launch and sat on this shingle, the only thing to move her would be the next swell coming in, this would then be too late, it would throw her broadside and smash her to pieces. Without beach help to lay woods out into the surf as far as possible during launch it was going to be a risky task.

"Right o Tom." he shouted ." lets get her ready, we'll wait until the flood gets hold of her and see how it looks then, if its died down a bit we'll have a go."

Setting about greasing the woods and making ready to launch, both of us knowing what to do, we made ready, and settled back against the hull of the boat to enjoy a few puffs on a thinly rolled cigarette. Quiet and motionless we waited, staring seaward without a word passing through our lips.

Watching the moon with the clouds drifting over it, like big feather dusters, my mind quickly drifted away into the dreams of ambition, like most of us did when in our younger years.

Looking into the unknown future of expectation; what I could do with a good season's wages. Walking through the reality of my own house, and a garden to plant a few flowers in; such dreams.

Before I realized it there was a booming of a loud voice in my right ear

"Wake up Tom! Come on wake up Tom! There's no time for sleeping now

I must have drifted away for quite some time, as on opening my eyes, and finding myself still leaning over the gunwales. I had fallen asleep standing on my two feet.

By now the wind had freshened and was blowing strong from the sou-west again, carrying the clouds fast and low across the sky; the sea shining up in the moonlight looked wild and foreboding, but the swell had been all but calmed down by the rush of the flood tide, now at its strongest.

"Don't look bad now skipper, does it? Are we going to have a try?"

"Yes Tom." came the reply." That's if you can keep awake long enough." he sniggered, as he took another deep drag on his cigarette, lighting the end of his red nose up with the sudden glare.

"Should be able to get afloat pretty easy now Tom, there's only the odd thumper rolling in, and we can see them in the moonlight coming from the pier head."

Sure enough the swells had quietened down enough to try a launch, apart from the odd thumper, as we call it, which was running right up the beach and gracing the stern of the boat with a kind of gentleness, leaving glittering droplets of water dripping from the keel, sparkling in the moonlight as they fell onto the beach below.

"How are we going to get the lower woods down skipper? Those thumpers will wash them away if we aren't smart off with the launching?"

."I know Tom, we've got to have those lower woods to get her afloat or we're sure as done for; tie them together Tom, dig the ends in the shingle and lets hope none of them get washed away."

I tied the woods together and started to lay them at four foot intervals behind the boat, going as far down the beach as possible, with the last one left loose. Next instant the sound of a thudding engine could be heard, the skipper had started her up.

."How you doing Tom, are you ready yet?" was the shout from the top of the beach.

What was about to happen now was a feat of skill and perfect timing, one mistake and we would be in great danger. The skipper would hold the slip release link on the reeving chain, watching the seas as they rolled shoreward, when the time was right he would let go, as we say, the chain would free and the boat would rush rapidly seaward, the skipper jumping in as soon as he had let go.. Me! I had to stay near the waters edge and place the lower wood as she rushed past into the water, hopefully jumping aboard as she sped past me, and trusting my skill and judgment to gain a hold on the gunwales to pull myself inboard so that I didn't fall back into the sea, it was no good shouting for help if I missed or didn't get a good hold, it would be tough luck, but we had both done this procedure many times before, and knew the thoughts of each other.

"Alright skipper, I'm ready down here." I shouted as I dug the lower wood hard into the shingle.

"Ok Tom, watch for the calm, and don't miss with that there last wood or we're done for." came the reply.

The minutes seemed like hours whilst waiting for that command, which would be." Let Go!" With every large sea washing the woods out of place and soaking me in the bargain, but quickly I continued replacing them back in their positions each time, I was instantly ready for the launch

A large sea came rushing up the beach almost knocking me off my feet, when the shout came.

"Let go!" The skipper had let go on the retreat of this large sea, knowing that there would be a calm following.

As the boat came rushing past me I threw the last wood into the shingle; just in time, the keel came over the bank and hit it like a railway engine hitting the buffers, crash, quickly she rushed past; instantly letting go of the lanyard which was holding the wood., I made a rapid jump for the gunwales, holding on for dear life as the boat hit the sea. In a split second the boat was heaving high in the air as the next large sea broke beneath her, we were afloat but not clear.

Meanwhile, struggling to raise myself over the gunwales I got yet a further soaking as the spray from the next sea that came shoreward and broke just ahead of our bows completely covered me, with the engine roaring full astern, we slowly pulled clear of the surf.

"Get back here astern Tom." came the command from the skipper." Put a bit more weight in the stern and get that prop biting."

Rushing astern, I positioned myself on the aft thwart taking straight to the pump, as during the launch much water had been taken over the side by the second large sea that came upon us. How we got afloat I don't know.

Having been pulled clear enough of the shore the rudder was shipped and ahead gear selected, the helm was put hard over and her head turned toward the pier head, I carried on pumping until the water was bought down to a safe level. We had made it, a bit of soaking but we made it, now all that was hoped for was a good catch of herring to make the evening worth while. God had been with us so far.

****

CHAPTER TWO

THE DRIFT

    Unhurriedly we made our way out to the pier head, which lay but some six hundred yards off shore from the beach plot. The swells, still rolling in heavily, lifted us high in the air, so that we could see all the houses down the side streets, their roofs shining brightly in the beams of the full moon, then as we wallowed into the following trough all view of the land was obliterated, even though it was but a few hundred yards away, giving the sensation that any moment we would come to grinding halt, hitting the sea bed before being lifted by the next swell.

"Alright Tom?" came the booming voice of the skipper across the roar of the wind and the engine." Aye skipper got a bit of a soaking but otherwise alright." I replied.

"The swells picking up again Tom, there's still a lot more wind to come yet I recon." Said the Skipper

    I should by this time mention that the skipper's name was Harry, although every body along the foreshore called him "Skipper." why I am not certain, but most of the boatmen had some form of nickname, acquired by a past feat that had its fortune to be bestowed on them.

    By now the wind had increased considerably, and the swells beneath us were gathering tremendous force again.

"Looks like we got afloat just in time skipper." I shouted," another half an hour and we'd be stuck ashore me thinks, what'll you reckon skipper?"

    Turning his head towards the shore and then looking out to sea into the oncoming swells, he slowly turned to me and nodded his head.

"Right enough Tom, not a minute too early, but we're here now; let's worry about getting back ashore when the time comes. Get the pole end dhan ready Tom."

The pole end dhan was a small flag pole with corks tied a third the way up its length, on the bottom of the pole was an iron weight, at the top was a flag. When dropped into the water the flag would float upright, thus allowing us to see where the end of the nets are. The pole end is the first end to be cast into the sea, with the dhan attached.

As we reached the pier head, the skipper slowed the engine's revs, and then knocked her out of gear, looking around; the sea was glistening with all kinds of lights coming from the vessels that were anchored in the Downs for shelter.

"Well skipper." I shouted." Look at that lot, there's hardly enough room for a drive tonight is there?"

A drive is the term used for a long drift, once the nets are in the sea they drift with the tide for two or three miles before being hauled.

"Aye looks pretty crowded don't it, looks like we'll have to shoot them down stream and see if we can drive between these ships Tom."

Usually the nets were shot across the tide, but owing to the amount of shipping lying at anchor, drifting room was limited, so shooting with the tide was the only other option,

As far as the eye could see there were hundreds of ships anchored, much closer to the shore than we expected, a large full rigged ship was approaching us from the sou'ard, making some fifteen knots, top and mizzen billowing out before her as she rushed before the wind and tide, what a beautiful craft. All through the Downs vessels were maneuvering for a position to anchor in, lit by the moonlight, the scene was spectacular to view, although not a good sign for us with a mile of drift nets to shoot away.

Large silhouettes could be seen in the flash of the East Goodwin Lightship as ships passed across its beam, giving a glimpse to all of the size and sail of these beautiful vessels.

"She hasn't seen us Tom, hang on."

The skipper threw the helm shoreward and opened up the engines revs. A large sailing vessel just cleared the pier, and came down upon us without warning, almost scraping the varnish from our stern.

"That were close skipper." I shouted as the vessel continued its course towards Sandown Castle. ."I never saw her coming, too busy looking seaward

"Well Tom, I think that we'll shoot part the way out pier head, looks pretty clear along shore, keep those buoys tucked under the head-lines as you go Tom."

The herring nets had large cork buoys tied to the top head line at intervals of four fathoms; these were attached by two fathom ropes which could be tied at various lengths, allowing the nets to float close to the surface or nearer the sea bed. As we were shooting close inshore and the depth was shallow the buoys were tide up tight, keeping the nets higher off the sea bed.

Pulling up to the third shelter on the pier, we stopped, the rudder was shipped and the mizzen set, two long twelve foot oars were set in the rowlocks astern. Then the powerful arms of the skipper started rowing her stern first down with the wind and tide, slowly she started to gather way. I stood by the midship thwart, waiting for instructions, with the pole end dhan in my hand.

"Right oh! Let 'er go Tom," shouted the skipper in my ears.

The dhan was lowered over the side, with the boat going in astern it quickly floated away from the side of the boat pulling the head-line overboard as the tide got hold of it. Rapidly I started paying out the lead line, throwing overboard the buoys as they came upon me. One by one and net by net the gear went over the side.

"Slow down a bit skipper," I shouted," my arms are dropping off."

With the wind on the port bow we were blowing out to sea too fast for me to keep up with the shooting.

"What's up Tom." boomed the skipper." Old age creeping up on you?"

It was alright for him, he only stood there pulling on the oars, but experience told me not to answer him back, for the fear of a clip round the ear coming my way.

Over and over they went, until the last buoy was thrown seaward, followed closely by the swing rope

This is the rope used to hold onto the nets, it's around ten fathoms long and one end is attached to the top of the nets, whilst the other is tied to the bow of the boat. The boat has a mizzen sail set aft and can now swing to and fro without leaving the nets.

Quickly making this fast around the Samson post, I threw myself on to the for'ard thwart* exhausted. Whilst down the stern, the skipper pulled in the large oars, tightened in the mizzen sheet and shipped the rudder. Round she came head to wind, pulling tight on the nets, steadying under the heave of the swells as the mizzen took the wind. At last they were over.

"That were a fast shoot skipper; I've got quite a sweat on now!" I exclaimed as I sat down on the thwart puffing rapidly almost out of breath.

He looked at me and smiled as he lit another cigarette, then turned his head to the nor'ard, assessing our position, and not saying a word for many minutes, but just staring in to the darkness with a sort of a solemn quietness.

What was going through that learned mind of his could only be imagined, and would later more than likely be revealed.

Looking north towards Ramsgate the sea showed up as a mass of glittering lights, ships anchored as far as the eye could see, riding out the storms that had been prevailing over the last few days, and the way the wind was gusting again it was not by a long shot over yet.

Broken water constantly gave us an unwelcome wash every time she rolled to port, and the swells were starting to run toward the beach even heavier, with breaking heads of creamy white foam rolling over their tops, the roar of their pounding upon the beach could be heard above the wind, some half a mile off shore.

"Jump to it Tom." cried the skipper." There's a damned Barque anchored straight in our path, running totally black."

This is an expression for a ship with no lights showing.

In an instant the skipper had the engine running, and I had bent* the hurricane lamp onto the dhan, which I then tied to the swing rope and made ready to let go.

"Alright Tom, let it go, dammed silly so and so's." the skipper muttered." Too bone idle to raise an anchor lamp, deserve to get run down."

Having let go of the nets and marked them with the light we turned towards the Barque, making as much speed as possible. It wouldn't be long before the nets had drifted down on top of her, and then there'd be a mess.

A few minutes steaming and we had reached the Barque. The Charlotte was her name, from Biddeford.

"Ahoy there! Ahoy there Barque Charlotte! Any one onboard?" Bawled the skipper in somewhat of an angry voice.

There was no reply so again he shouted to the Barque to try and get some attention.

"Ahoy there you lazy good for nothing land lubbers get on deck."

An old seaman poked his head over the rail of the Barque, in a rather dazed and semi sleep manner, As soon as he appeared the skipper set about giving him ten pennith of the foulest language any one can imagine from an old Deal boatman. The poor chap onboard was taken by surprise and totally unaware as to what was going on.

"Where's your bloody riding light?" The skipper shouted. "How do you expect a soul to see you in these weather conditions without a bloody riding light? You deserve to get run down."

The skipper by now was rather concerned, and getting angry as well, without much more ado he threw the helm over and started making way back to the nets, which now were but a hundred yards away from fouling the Barque's anchor cable.

"Get that bloody knife ready Tom." he shouted as we came along side the nets." We're run along the head line and split the nets, that'll let them pass each side of the Barque's hull."

Angrily we picked up the head line and hung fast to it in the position where the ships cable was to run through it.

"Right Tom." he screamed." Cut the ties." As he said this I ran a knife down the lacings and separated the nets. A common practice in these circumstances.

"Just in time skipper." I shouted as we slid down the side of the Barque's hull, being watched from above by the crew who were by now all on deck.

Waving his fist at them and in a temper, he wasn't a man to argue with, he has been known to knock down the stoutest of fellows in a fight.

"I've a good mind to cut your bloody anchor away you lazy swabs, get your riding light up."

We slid quickly down the Barque's side rounding her stern; the nets were bought together again and quickly laced down, thus joining the fleet of gear back together.

Still shouting abuse at the Barque, which was quite out of earshot by now, the skipper turned to me and said?
"Did you see that Tom?"
"What's that skipper?" I answered
"Don't say your bloody blind as well, didn't you see?"

I was still unaware of what he was talking about, and cautiously answered for fear of a reprisal, as the skipper still had a temper running within him.

"No, what was it skipper?" I replied carefully.

"Bloody herring Tom, loads of bloody herring in the nets. Don't say you never saw them?"

During the confusion I had not noticed the fish in the nets, but he had, which to some degree had quietened him down.

"Pick up the swing rope Tom," he shouted as we came round on the dhan with its light on.

Grabbing hold I heaved it aboard, untied the dhan and made the swing rope fast
"Right oh!" I shouted. "All secure skipper."

."Good Tom lets have' a look on shall we." and with this I started to pull on the swing rope while the skipper slackened the mizzen sheet and got one of his large oars out over the side.

A look on is an expression used to haul a part of the net aboard to see if there are any fish swimming, the section of net is emptied then shot away again, this is done several times normally during a drift, and gives an idea as to when the fish have stopped swimming into the net.

Pulling the boat against the wind was a hard task; a good strong gale was now blowing, having swung more southerly, throwing showers of spray in all directions, adding that little extra bit of water to the inside of my oilskins and relieving any dry patch that happened to remain within.

Slowly the boat heaved up to the first net, the first buoy was pulled inboard, and the skipper pulled rapidly on the head line and picked up the lead line.   The nets swung out like a carpet abeam of us, some
fourty feet or so shining in the moonlight, what a sight!

"Look skipper!" I shouted." Look in there, it looks like we have found them tonight, haven't we?"

Pulling slowly on the ground-rope the skipper smiled and said nothing. Half a net was hauled then let to go over the side again, being relieved of its catch as it was reshot.

"Right oh Tom, make fast the swing rope." was the order from the stern as the skipper put the large oar away and hauled in taught on the mizzen sheet

Meanwhile I had started to count the herring we had on board and placed them in one of the empty boxes we were carrying. The fish were counted in fours, which are called warps, there being thirty warps to the hundred. Ninety eight warps skipper, good show eh? I recon we've got them alright tonight haven't we?" I shouted excitedly.

"Aye not bad Tom, but the tide hasn't finished yet, we're only off Sandown castle, plenty of tide to run yet."

"I recon at this rate we should see three or four last tonight, that'll make them jump on the shore skipper, should get a good price too."

The skipper leaned over the midship thwart, and strained his eyes through the encrusted salt sticking to his face

"Good sizes too, aren't they? Nice and lively too, be plenty more swimming yet Tom, we'll have another look at the six green."

The wind had now swung right through southerly and increased to a good force nine throwing us about in all directions. Shipping was still coming into the Downs looking for a place to anchor, whilst others bound for the north, took advantage in the change of direction of the wind and made sail through the Gulls, and out into the next dangerous journey, the Thames Estuary with its multitude of sandbanks.

Turning my head to the south'ard momentarily, I saw a small two masted schooner bearing down on us, doing a fair turn of speed and running on reefed sail

"Skipper! Look there: she's going to run straight through our gear at that course." I shouted, pointing in the direction of the vessel.

He jumped to his feet quickly to see what the fuss was about, put his hand over his forehead to stop the spray hitting his eyes, and stared into the direction that I was pointing.

"Damned fool!" he shouted." He'll not only run us through but he will go aground shortly if he doesn't alter tack, come on Tom lets go chase him."

Once again the engine was started and the light tied to the swing rope.

. Ok let it go Tom." came the instructions.

The dhan was placed overboard, and with an instant the engine was running at full speed, her head was turned into the teeth of the gale towards the schooner.

Crash... tons of water went flying in all directions as our bows drove into the swells

"Get on the pump Tom, the waters over the floor boards." This wasn't surprising with the amount of sea coming over the gunwales.

It wasn't long before we heaved to on the schooner, which by now had relieved her mast of some of the strain and was running on jib and mizzen only, she was still turning a fair rate of knots though.

Hard over to starboard went our helm as the skipper ran the boat alongside the schooner, which was the Jasper from Cardiff?

."Ahoy there matey, you're running into danger." Bellowed the skipper as loud as he could over the roaring wind.

. What's up mate?" Came the reply from a seaman on the schooner's deck.

"We've got a half mile of drifting net ahead of you mate, you won't be able to stand on this course." replied the skipper.

."Thanks mate." came the reply." We're bound for London and are seeking shelter out of this sea. Its mountainous half mile further out, no where to anchor with all these head of sail in here, any ideas?"

The skipper instantly saw his chance and forgetting the herring nets set about another task.

."We will be alright here Tom?" He said. ."Here, take the helm and put me on board her."

I knew what he was up to and if it paid off we'd be a bit worse for wear by the time we got ashore.

Running alongside the schooner and closing up to her bulkwards, the skipper clambered aboard her." Pick me up in a few minutes Tom; stay close, don't fall back too far now, and keep your eyes on the nets." He yelled as he disappeared out of sight.

Pulling away from the schooner I kept in hailing distance, the schooner came round to wind'ard, with sails falling to the deck as her head took the bight of the wind. The anchor chain was run free, disturbing the wail of the wind with its clanging and rattling as it sped towards the sea bed. She's down and fast, I thought.

Turning the boat's head toward the wind I made my way back to the schooner, the skipper was waiting at the rail for me.

"Bring her in Tom." he shouted.

As I brought the boat alongside the schooner the skipper jumped aboard, followed by two small kegs.

"You'll be safe there matey, there's plenty of water at bottom tide to float you." he shouted to the chap on the schooner as he left her.

And with this he took the helm from me and paid off.

"So long mates, God's speed go with you.

The schooner was left behind, and a course set back to the nets, the light of which could hardly be seen through the flying spray.

"There it is skipper a couple of points to port, look; over there!"

Turning towards the light we made rapid speed and soon came up on it, round she came, up into the wind.

"Have you got it Tom?"

"Aye skipper, she's in."

I pulled the dhan in and made the swing rope fast to the Samson post, up came the boat's head with a jolt, straining the rope so much that the water was completely rung out of it

"All secure skipper," I shouted.

Settling down in the bottom of the boat, somewhat exhausted from breathing in so much salt water spray, and the boat continuing the drift once more, my thoughts went to the two casks that the skipper had brought aboard from the schooner.

"Well." said the skipper." You are properbly wondering what's in them there casks aren't you?"

"Aye that I am skipper."

."Well the seamen on the schooner thanked me for saving their ship from going aground and blessed me with two casks of brandy, a small reward in the least for saving their ship. Don't you think Tom?"

He had given some tall story to frighten the poor fellows to death as usual, convincing them that only he could save their ship from doom, and being tossed upon an open beach with no hope of rescue, the crew, having thus rewarded him with the brandy.

"A bit more money in your pocket when we get ashore Tom, we'll sell them in the pub."

I knew full well what he was going to do, so didn't argue with him, and as the squeak of a cork hit my ears followed by a somewhat gurgling voice, my suspicions were confirmed.

"Well, that's the best swag I have tasted for many a day." He said joyfully as another mouthful of the intoxicating liquid slid down his throat.

He would be drunk within the next half hour if I wasn't mistaken. Settling back into the bow, I watched in auger as he slowly consumed mouthful after mouthful of the prime Napoleonic brandy, he was however just as good a seaman drunk as he was sober, sometimes better to say the least, so there was no fear about his condition.

The next ten minutes seemed to go by more like an hour, with the wind whistling through the rigging on the fore-mast followed by the musical accompaniment of the skipper, singing at the top of his voice, and staggering somewhat from side to side seemingly finding great difficulty in holding the deck which was rolling and pitching heavily.

Spray was being thrown over us continuously now; and the tide had eased, thus allowing the swells to build up to their full capacity, with curling tops being brushed off by the strong wind.

"Let's have a look Tom!" came the muffled cry from the stern, as once again he fell against the gunwales and nearly pitched himself overboard.

"Ready when you are skipper," I shouted, gathering another mouthful of water as a large sea broke over our bow.

Steadily I pulled in the swing rope, and getting the headline aboard, made the first buoy fast around the forward thwart. Pulling with all my might on the headline, the footrope was soon reached and passed astern.

"Here you are skipper, grab a hold. Got it.?"
He grabbed the foot rope of the herring net and smiled.

"Right oh! Tom." he shouted." Let's have a look."

Hauling commenced with the strain of pulling the boat up to the nets against this wind, an almost impossible task.

"Can't get much way on her skipper." I shouted as another sea hit the bow of the boat, almost blinding us with stinging spray, which condescended to fill my mouth again with another unwanted cupful of salty water. ."The wind and sea's getting a bit heavy skipper."

"Just do your best Tom, just do your best, there's no hurry to get ashore, bloody swells are going in like mountains, we'll wait till low water, it'll be quieter then, keep pulling Tom."

The first three buoys were now aboard, about half a net, my arms felt like they were being pulled out of their sockets, as I tried my hardest to pull the nets in against the strength of wind and sea.

"What'll you recon on that Tom?" shouted the skipper in a slightly undecernable tone of voice.

"Looks mighty pretty doesn't it skipper, Looks like we are going to get a good haul if they keep coming in like this, eh?"

"Aye Tom, they's getting thicker aren't they?"

The nets were glowing in the moonlight as it passed from behind a cloud, shining as though someone had sewn thousands of sequins to them; we had struck fish and a good size too.

Slowly and painfully we hauled the gear, the buoys coming aboard one at a time, the sea surging into white crests came steadily rolling over our beam, the stinging spray hitting us full on in the face, like sharp splinters of flying glass.

"Make fast Tom." came the order from the stern, as the skipper fell against the aft thwart."I've got to have a quick pump out, the waters up over the deck level."

Securing the headline to the forward mast, I fell back on to the thwart, exhausted from the strain of hauling in such severe conditions.

"Are you alright Tom?" cried the skipper

"Aye just about skipper, bloody arms are dropping off though, the sea's getting rougher, and the strain is getting worse, but I'll manage."

Pulling away at the pump handle, with a staggering and rolling motion, the skipper slowly managed to get the water level down in the bilges. Much cursing was coming from the stern, every time she rolled the water from the pump was blown back into the skipper's face, soaking him from top to bottom, relieving him of words that would not be polite for me to repeat.

"Ok Tom, let's get them in." Once more we started to haul the nets aboard, with fish coming over the rail in their scores.

Buoy after buoy came aboard, the weight of the fish getting heavier all the time.

"She's getting low in the water skipper with all the weight aboard her? Do you think we'll carry them all?"

"Aye looks good don't she, don't you worry Tom, we've got another foot or more of free board on her yet, keep them darlings coming in."

Continuing with the task in hand I said no more, each sea seemingly getting heavier, trying with my strongest effort to pull the nets aboard, every wave grabbing at the nets and half pulling me overboard, my arms being almost drawn out of their sockets with every jerk. The last net had been reached, the strain of a fleet of nets hanging from the boat was eased, and she slowly blew round broadside to the sea and wind. In came the pole end dhan followed closely by the last buoy.

"Thank God for that," I shouted as I fell onto the thwart. "That was bloody hard going."

I looked at the pile of nets that was stacked up amidships, some three feet above the gunwale level, shining silver with the catch they contained.

"A good catch skipper, but its put us low in the water hasn't it? Its not going to be an easy job beaching."

"Don't you worry Tom." was the reply from the stern as another cup of brandy went down the already half pickled hatch of the skipper's throat, followed by a large gulp and comments of; how refreshing that was.

"We will go ashore at low tide, it'll be daylight then and hopefully the swells will have dropped away."

On this part of the beach in a southerly wind the swells always lost their height and power as the tide fell away, though they could still be a hazard, they were nothing like the huge seas that roared in two hours before, and two hours after the high tide.

Settling down in the stern the skipper started to pump out the bilges again, then the engine was started, mizzen sail hauled taught, ahead gear engaged on the engine and slowly and heavily the boat's head came up to the wind.

By this time we were midway betwixt the B1 and B2 banks, with around four fathoms of water, some four miles distance from Deal beach. These sand banks dried on a very low water and although they gave a certain amount of shelter at high tide, were a danger as the tide fell away, heavy broken seas would roll across them, capsizing any boat that should have the misfortune of trying to cross them,

Slowly the heavily laden boat gathered way, pitching heavily into every sea, taking most over the side.

"Come astern Tom." came the orders as the cup of brandy left his mouth for a minute." Come and get on this here pump, get some of that there water out of her."

Clambering over the nets I made my way to the stern, grasped the pump handle, and started pumping.

"She's heavy in water skipper, what'll you reckon we've got?" I asked him.

"About ten lasts I think looking at them, not a bad haul considering the weather, eh?"

A last was a thousand herring, some thirty stone; we had about three hundred stone of fish as well as the wet nets. Although low in the sea she was carrying them well, the weight keeping her steady as she drove into the oncoming seas, what a miracle this would be if we made it back to shore in one piece.

"We are only going slow Tom otherwise she might drive herself under with all this weight aboard, besides there's another three hours to low water, and it'll be breaking daylight by then."

A large ship was anchored to seaward of us flying an English pennant, straining heavily at her anchors, both of which had been dropped to hold her against the gale and force of the oncoming tide and seas.

"Look there Tom, it's a British merchantman, should be a bit of lee there."

The skipper had intentions of going alongside her and at once threw the tiller round turning our head towards the ship.

"Should give us a bit of lee for a couple of hours while we are waiting to beach Tom, get ready to go longside."

Grabbing a rope I made my way back to the bows, as the skipper brought us steadily alongside the huge wooden wall that lie here at anchor.

"Grab a hold of this rope mate, make her fast." shouted the skipper to a seaman who was looking over the ship's side that towered above us.

I threw the rope to him and quickly we were made fast along side the ship. It was quite calm on her lee side as she was swung slightly across the tide which had now ebbed.

The man lowered a rope ladder down over the ship's side from which in no time the skipper was ascending.

"Stay here Tom and keep an eye on the boat, don't let her bang about too much, I wont be long." and away he went up the rope ladder, leaving me below.

The minutes seemed like hours with the wind blustering and the seas becoming whiter crested as the tide ran ebb, now in full force against the southerly gale, it was going to be some time before the skipper came back, so paying out some more line, I let the boat run away from the ship's side a bit further, aiding somewhat in the arduous task of fending off. This took away the shelter I was getting from the lee of the ship and caused me to maintain a constant hand on the pump, drawing out the water which was rolling over the beam ends. Settling down on the aft thwart and working the pump at a steady rate, I prepared for a long and tedious wait.

Daylight was just starting to break, lighting the horizon for some miles in a dull crimson red, the wind swept clouds ran rapidly across the sky as if they had no time to lose in reaching their destination and dropping the odd squally shower as they passed. With visibility improving I could make out every ship lying in the Downs.

There must be at least two hundred head of sail anchored as far as the eye could see, leaving no space for any more, others were running through the Gulls north bound taking advantage of the improved conditions now the tide had fallen, others south bound were rolling heavily at their cables as every swell lifted them broadside on, making life on board very uncomfortable. The Goodwins were sending pillars of water high in the air as the heavy sea pounded upon them, silhouetting the vessels anchored between them and us. A moment's glance to the sou'east took my attention, no! I was dreaming, most probably too much salt in my eyes;

I looked again to the sou'east rubbing the salt and spray from my eyes as I did, it was, yes it was!

Some four miles distant in amongst the breakers on the sands could be made out the distinct shape of a two masted ship, having had the misfortune to drag her anchors and go aground, a fire was burning on deck showing smoke only, that's why we hadn't seen her in the dark. The position was not good; she was listing badly to the nor'east and with the falling tide wouldn't be long going to pieces. A quick glance round to the shore gave sight to what I had expected, the distress fire had been seen on the beach, and some half a dozen head of sail were racing seaward under heavy canvas towards the stricken vessel. The Deal boatmen were on their way.

A chance of easy salvage money was within reach and here we were with a boat load of herring, unable to try our hand at gaining some booty from the ill fated vessel, sure; if we'd stayed ashore nothing would have gone aground, but then the money was sure with the catch we had, shouldn't like the thought of trying to go alongside in this sea anyway.

I watched for about an hour as several more boats left the beach to the stricken vessel, by now it was only just visible through the huge seas which were breaking over its hull, both the masts having been carried away. The fire had been extinguished on the deck and several small sails could be seen around her. They must have managed to get alongside I thought, otherwise they wouldn't be lying like they were with just their mizzens blowing. It seemed as though I had been watching all day as the minutes flew past and my thoughts were running to the rescue of those poor souls aboard, some of which were sure never to see another day, but then if that's how God wants it, there's no hiding.

My arm was aching badly from the pumping and I was just thinking about how long it would be before the skipper would return, when, from above me came the bellowing voice of the skipper himself.

"Ahoy down there in that old fishing boat, get alongside and pick me up Tom."

Hanging over the rail was the reddened face of the skipper, unusually none the worst for wear, this wasn't like him after a spell on board a ship, I was expecting to see him being lowered back into our boat legless and very drunk.

I pulled the boat alongside fending off as the seas picked her up and tried to throw her against the wooden wall, over the rail came the skipper. He rapidly climbed down the rope ladder. I looked at him amazed, he wasn't drunk.

"What's up Tom?" he shouted." Seen a ghost?" he said sniggering loudly to himself.

"No skipper it's………."

"I know, you thought I was going be blind drunk didn't you? Well I'm not, get that there basket out of the bows and fill her with some herring."

I pulled a quarter cran basket out of the forepeak and filled it with herring as ordered.

"What do you want them for skipper?" I asked, not that I hadn't already guessed.

He hooked the basket of herring to the rope that was hanging down from the ship's side

"Right oh matey, haul her up." he shouted to a crewman on the ship above us.

The basket was hoisted up over the ship's side, emptied and lowered down again.

"Careful Tom." he shouted." Don't let it bang against the side."

The basket came aboard and was unhitched, the rope being pulled up over the rails of the ship and disappearing out of sight.

"Here, get this stuff stowed under the footings Tom, no one will see it there; we'll get it out at dark tonight."

The basket was full of bottles of rum, some score of them.

"Not a bad deal eh Tom? A bit more money in our pockets eh?"

With the bottles stowed below the footings we were ready to head for shore. The mizzen was reset to hold her steady and the engine started.

"So long mate's safe journey." he shouted to the crew of the ship.

."Ok Tom cast off."

Lines away, we blew clear from the ships side rounded her stern and opened up to the full fury once more of the sea and wind, white water was everywhere. Her head went into the wind and a slow way set towards the pier head.

"Get on this pump Tom; keep her dry, it's going to be a bit of a wet trip."

It sure was, every sea she hit was throwing itself high up over the bows, only to come cascading inboard again, keeping the bilges full of water, and making my arms ache even more as I worked the pump handle frantically to and fro.

."Here look at that Tom, what are all those boats doing out there beyond the fork spit, something going on?"

"Yes skipper there's a ship gone aground on the sands, must be at least a dozen boats gone to her aid, it happened about two hours ago."

"Damn." shouted the skipper." Of all the luck and here we are stuck with a load of herring. Of all the things to happen, still can't do much about it now, lets get ashore before the tide makes."

With his eyes glaring at the stricken vessel and cursing under every breath about the bounty lost, he once again set a course for the pier.

****

CHAPTER THREE

ASHORE AT LAST

The steam back to shore was only about a mile and a half distant, although not without some scary moments. The weight of herring we had on board left us very low in the water, every sea that hit us on the port bow rolled over the fore peak and into the bilges, not giving me any rest from the rocking to and fro of the pump handle.

The ebb tide running south against the wind caused the seas to become broken with white curling tops on each one; instead of the heavy large swells thundering shore wards, which is more common to the slack and high water. The odd sea did come our way however, on a couple of occasions the heavy laden boat just ploughed her head straight into a broken wave crashing deep into the one following it, almost filling her to sinking level, shaking and shivering as though she had had enough and wanted to end the strain of her burden. But rapidly the pump released the water, only to have another lump come topside and fill the bilges again.

As we approached the pier head at the top of King Street we met what we hoped we wouldn't. Large broken seas were running the length of the pier towards the shore, a very dangerous position to be in under normal circumstances in an open boat, let alone one heavy in the water with fish. The shore had become busy with boatmen rushing up and down preparing the way for us to land. This was one asset at least, we had some help ashore, although be it many were just curious to see what we had caught.

The skipper laid the boat too just outside the pier head for several minutes, watching each wave as it rushed rapidly towards the shore, leaving a trail of glistening white foam in its wake.

"Don't look like we'd be able to live in that water." cried the skipper." It's too darn broken, we'd get swallowed up in one of them there troughs."

The head of the boat was turned eastward and the decision made to lie to for a while, giving the tide a chance to rise, this would stop the broken seas running. But as the tide rose the swells would become heavier again. Not much of a choice anyway we looked at it.

Half an hour passed with the seas still running heavy shore wards, and the tide having risen, the crests had all but disappeared.

"Right oh Tom!" exclaimed the skipper." We're going to have a go."

He waved his arm to the men on the shore to make sure all was ready; a wave of acknowledgement came back. All was ready ashore.

"Reeve the chain Tom, we're going in."

The reeving chain was a long length of chain passed through the ruffle hole in the keel at the bow; it was pulled through by a small rope and joined by a hook, the purpose of its being is it's used to haul the boat up the beach.

The chain reeved, the skipper headed for the shore, the poor old Kelvin engine running as hard as it could, giving us all of four knots. In she went, picking up speed and slowing down again as she was picked up by the seas running beneath her keel. So far so good, a large sea appeared at the pier head towering above all the others, the curling foamy white crest breaking over itself as it rushed towards us.

"Look skipper there's a thumper coming in." the skipper turned his head seaward, viewing the sea and gave an expression of awe.

"Can't do much about it now Tom, by the time we turn she'll hit us abeam and overwhelm us, just have to hitch onto her and let her have us."

No sooner had he said this than the stern was picked up and the sea broke under our midships, speed increased and the skipper holding fast to the tiller, steered her straight towards the beach

"Hang on Tom we're going in now, too late to change your mind."

With lightening speed the boat rushed towards the beach, foaming sea breaking all around us; with a loud crash we struck the shore, with tons of water rushing turbulently over our gunwales. She stuck fast on the beach, the weight of the fish and the water being too much to let her float off again.

Quickly the winch wire was hooked up and the strain taken, with two men on each handle of the winch putting every ounce behind their effort to wind the boat clear of the surf.
Being so heavily laden the risk of damage was increased, as the sea would smash her up if she didn't lay lively in the hitch.

Slowly the strain came upon her, creaking and groaning she lifted her head onto the first greased wood, inching her way out of the surf, she slid up onto the second wood healing over on her port beam and letting some of the sea water out over her rail. One of the beach hands dived under her stern to pull out the bung thus releasing the water trapped within her hull; he took the full force of a sea as it rushed up the beach beneath her, soaking every part of him

"Did you get it out me old brancher?" shouted the skipper, as the poor drenched fella stood up and shook himself.

"Aye old fella." came the reply as the helper shoved the cork down the aft thwart for safety.

Now clear of the sea the order was given to stop hauling and allow the water to drain from the bilges, making the boat lighter to haul up the beach.

"Morning skipper." came a voice from behind.

It was one of the older boatmen who had been watching the whole procedure from the covering seats on the seafront.

."Didn't expect to see you away last night old fella, bit of a blow on wasn't there?"

"Certainly was mi old brancher." replied the skipper." Lot a sea running outside, we had to move a couple a small vessels that run down our way, otherwise all went well."

."Got a good haul old fella haven't you, done alright for yourself today, you should fetch a pretty penny too, none on the market you know, no-one else has been afloat, except to that there ship aground on the fork spit, I don't give much on their hopes though, a lot of sea breaking over her, bad do."

"Aye me old brancher, I suppose we're lucky to get a haul, at least it's a wage. Right oh mates haul away," the skipper shouted as he slid another board under the boat's bow.

The water had drained from the bilges and hauling once more commenced, slowly she raised her bow up over the high water bank and came to rest on the stocks placed at the edge of the promenade.

"Hold it mates, make her fast." shouted the skipper. The pool on the winch went with a clang as it took the strain of the boat, stopping it from making a return seaward.

"Make her fast Tom, come on you lot." he shouted to the beach help." We haven't got all day, let's get the canvas down and get these here fish shook out."

With the boat all secure, a large canvas was spread out on the beach to catch the herring as they were shaken out of the nets, making it easier for us to pick up and box them, as well as stopping them from becoming covered in dirt from the stones.

Normally the nets would be skilled onto long poles lying on the beach, in order that they can dry in the wind and thus preventing rotting, but owing to the severe weather conditions that had been prevailing these had been taken down and the nets safely stowed in the boat, should the need for a quick rescue be required if the sea came up too far. The nets were held in four positions, myself on the foot line or bottom, the skipper on the head rope and one man each end behind us to clear the nets from the catch as they came out of the boat.

Shaking out started, no mean task, and adding further to the already aching hands and arms I had from pumping out the boat. Over the gunwale they came, yard by yard, like thick silvery ropes, some herring dropping out into the boat and others falling on the canvas. Those still in were vigorously shaken out onto the canvas, some minus their heads owing to the strength with which they had hit the net.

Yard after yard and herring by the hundreds, scales flying through the air like glistening sequins falling on everyone and everything that got in their flight path, and still the fish kept coming.

By now a crowd was gathering, most of whom were waiting to buy the herring, others were watching in amazement at the fish we had caught.

"Hang on a minute Tom, I've got to get some of the weight out of the boat before it starts to tear the nets." the skipper ordered.

We all stopped and grabbing the boxes started to count the herring in to them, some from the canvas and some from within the boat, as many had fallen inside and were making it difficult to draw the rest of the nets from her well.

"Get in Tom." shouted the skipper." Put a hundred in each box." I climbed into the boat, followed sharply by several boxes which narrowly missed my head.

"Steady on mate's watch where you are throwing them there boxes." I bellowed out as two more came flying over the rail.

"What's up Tom can't you keep up the pace, we haven't got all day you know," answered the skipper.

I instantly kept quiet and set about the job of filling the boxes, knowing if I were to answer him back a few more boxes would suddenly come flying over the rail and land close or on top of me.

Each box was filled with thirty warps of herring, a warp being four, this making one hundred and twenty fish to the hundred. It was an old custom to sell by the hundred and throw in an extra twenty for nothing, it would allow for the gillers that would be in the count. These fish were not much use to the fish buyers as they had had their gills broken in the process of shaking them from the nets, the buyers said they couldn't smoke them as they wouldn't take to the smoking spits. Something I knew different as my father was a fish salesman and purchased many of the herring caught on the beach. I always managed to spit these herrings up for bloatering. I used an iron spit much thinner than a wooden one, so nothing was wasted. Still thirty warp was what they required and thirty warp they got.

The old timer who was leaning on the starboard bow started talking to the skipper whilst boxing was going on; the conversation of which I put myself out to hear, well you never knew what he was planning otherwise.

"Tell me skipper, what'll you be doing riding behind that ship down there, that one off Sandown Castle, you weren't in trouble were you?" He said with a smile on his face.

"No mi old brancher, it was just a bit of shelter me and Tom were seeking, whilst we let the tide run down a bit, didn't want to weather it out in the open sea, we thought it a good opportunity to have a bit a shelter, why?"

"Oh just curious skipper, thought you might have a bottle or two on board, no harm in asking is there?"

Looking up at them both I hesitated for a moment from what I was doing, the skipper looked at me with that look of surprise, and reading his face I knew instantly not to mention anything about what we had onboard, it would be more than my life was worth

"What'll you know old timer, you haven't seen anything you shouldn't, have you," he said to the old boatmen.

"Why no skipper! Only that…….."

"Only that what, old fella: what is it you have on your mind? Come on, let's be having it."

The old boatman smiled cunningly,

"Well skipper!" he exclaimed. ."When the other boats were launching to go to the aid of that stricken vessel on the fork spit, I was leaning here against the boathouse, and casually glancing out to sea through my telescope, just curious you know, looking at the other ships. Well you never know, one might need assistance, and with all the activity centered on the vessel in distress, it could easily go unnoticed. Well I got to wondering where you had gone; after all, I didn't want anything to happen to you. I was scanning the sea when I saw your boat drift out from astern of that large ship off Sandown Castle. Funny I thought myself, why would you be in her lee side all that time, when you could have come ashore quite easily? There was quite a few souls hanging over her deck as well, didn't fall in by any chance, did you skipper?"

"What do you mean old timer? I'm not that clumsy. What did you see that takes your fancy so easy then?"

The old boatman gave out a shifty giggle, then started laughing under his chin, raising his head and looking directly at the skipper, eyes straight and a sudden serious gleam replacing the humorous pose, he pulled the skippers bluff.

"It won't take much to keep me quiet skipper! Besides, the customs officers are on their way to see you; I heard it in passing The Compasses Arms a short while ago. Guess they are as curious as I am."

"Why didn't you say so." said the skipper somewhat panicking. ."You know what we have aboard, don't you? You old devil. So why the heck didn't you just tell me earlier?"

With out any hesitation the skipper quietly whispered to me.

"Get those bottles and casks out of the boat Tom, and hide them in the boxes under the herring, quickly now, there's no time to waste. Sprinkle a few herring on top of the boxes, and make sure you know which ones the goods are in. We don't want them going astray now."

I lifted up the floorboards of the boat, and carefully started to bring the bottles of Brandy out from their hiding place, placing two bottles in a box and covering them with herring, then passing the box out of the boat to the skipper and the helpers, who mixed them amongst the already boxes of herring lying on the beach. When all the bottles and the two casks had been removed and concealed, the job of shaking out continued.

"Hurry Tom; let's get these boxes loaded on the cart and away out of here."

"Old timer! If you help to take these boxes of herring to Tom's father's yard, there will be one in it for you; ok?"

The old timer nodded contentedly, and started to load the boxes of herring onto the hand cart. Several trips were made to my father's yard, and the boxes of fish stacked up by the smoke house door, ready for father to sort out. He knew what the position was and what he had to do with any booty he found concealed in the fish boxes.

"How many more full ones have you got that need to be taken Tom?" asked the skipper?

"Only two skippers, just about finished this lot now." I replied as I topped up another box and stacked it by the barrow.

The last box was loaded onto the hand cart, and the old boatman left to push it away on his own.

"You know what to do old timer, don't you?" Watch them well." Said the skipper as the old timer pushed the cart across the road.

The old boatman nodded agreeably and proceeded to push the cart and its contents away, he could always be trusted, as he had been in this situation on many occasions.

"Right mates, lets get the rest of these nets shook out before dark sets in upon us." The skipper shouted, as he bent down and picked up the lead line, commencing to shake the nets before he even straightened up.

Shaking out once more under full swing, slowly and steadily the nets came out of the boat and were relieved of their catch, the pile of fish on the canvas growing larger every minute.

Less than two nets had been cleared since the old boatman had left with his last cart of fish for my father's yard, when who should turn up but the customs men.

"Keep your mouths shut men; don't you let on to what we've been up to; you've seen and know nothing, Ok? I'll see you all alright in the pub tonight." the skipper said.

"Alright!" came the reply from all the helpers at once, as they continued innocently shaking out the herring.

Three customs men approached the boat, one leaned over the bows and looked inside, the other two positioned themselves, one by the skipper and one by my side, We never uttered a word to them, and likewise for several minutes they just stood there, motionless and quiet, watching as our work went on.

I watched the skipper through the corner of my eye as we continued shaking out the silver shining herring from the nets, suddenly a daze of unexpectation came across his face, and without warning, his voice bellowed out across the wind, drowning the noise of the surf breaking on the beach, and the whistling of the wind as it blew through the mesh's of the nets.

"Morning matey's, grand morning isn't it? He roared.

There was silence for a minute, an awful awe was running across our bows; no one uttered a word, once again the skipper shouted out.

"What's up matey's, lost your tongues, or are you expecting a feed of free herring. There's nothing here matey's that a shilling wont buy you, times are hard you know, if you're looking for a free feed, best you keep on moving."

Sniggering under his breath as he continued pulling on the nets and shaking out, even more vigorously, I could see that he was becoming rather angry, although he was trying not to show it.

"Hold on a bit skipper, I've only one pair of hands you know, let me catch up a bit, or are you forgetting that there's others shaking out here as well."

In his hidden temper of the customs officials being there he had forgotten about working as a team in shaking out, anger carrying him away, he was shaking so fast that we were unable to keep up with him.

Fearful of the response of shouting at him, and not knowing quite what to expect, I cautiously crouched to the ground, waiting for a large handful of herring to come flying through the air, directed at my head. The skipper didn't take kindly to being shouted at, especially from his crew. I received an angry glance, and then he turned his head and said nothing. Thank goodness for that, I thought, I shouldn't have reacted so fast on the skipper that was a close thing.

The customs officer at the bow of the boat ventured to speak the first words.

"Much more to go skipper?" He asked.

Silence struck the air again, then, after a minute or two the skipper responded.

"Should see the back of them in about ten minutes matey, there's only one net left to go now; you've got eyes in your head haven't you? You can see what left to shake out."

Silence sealed his lips again, unlike the skipper as he was always chatting about something. What was he thinking about? The customs officers couldn't prove anything, there's no evidence lying about, it's all gone, that's unless! No; they couldn't have found anything at my father's yard, surely they haven't had time to go there first.

"Not a bad catch today skipper is it?" exclaimed one of the customs officers, as he moved towards the boat and peered over its gunwale. ."Have a rough night did you?"

"No matey, not at all, bit of a breeze blowing but nothing we couldn't handle; been afloat in worse." The skipper replied.

."We watched you launch last night skipper, had a fair drive down didn't you?" he said. ."What happened this morning, loose your way did you?"

."What do you mean matey." The skipper replied. ."I've never lost my way out there, I know the sea like the back of my hand," he shouted disgustedly under his breath. ."Lost my way; huh, damn cheek."

The customs officer moved towards the stern of the boat then commented again.

"We saw you pull alongside that large three masted ship skipper, and then you disappeared for a good long while; a lot of activity on board her as well. What did you go alongside her for then?"

The Skipper, having been in this situation before, knew what was coming up, and what the customs men were trying to find out. He was quick and ready with an answer.

"Well matey, if you had looked hard enough through your glass's, you would have seen that we had a problem with the old engine, all that sea running out there went and flooded her. Some big old swells were coming aboard us you know. The only option was to make fast to the ship as she was close to us, so this we did. Good job she was anchored there or we'd have blown out to sea. We tied alongside her and those gracious seamen threw us some dry cloth to dry the engine out. Kind chaps made us a brew as well, quite a relief to get aboard her for a while. The engine dry we started up and made for shore again. Well that's the whole of the story mates, take it or leave it."

The skipper bent down and started picking up herring and filling the boxes, ignoring the comments made by the customs officer. He then turned to me and asking the same question, commented.

"Is that so Tom, and where were you during this so called drying out of the engine?"

"In the stern of the boat guv; pumping her bilges dry of the sea we had taken aboard whilst steaming, it's not calm out there you know. Weight of the fish and nets set us pretty low in the water guv, that's why we shipped so much; where else do you think I'd be? Taking a swim." I said annoyingly.

"Besides the skipper went aboard the ship to get some dry canvas to dry the engine out, I stayed aboard in case she broke adrift, wouldn't pay to leave the boat unmanned; Would it?"

"Well skipper." the other customs officer piped up. ."You didn't happen to bring any bottles of spirits ashore with you, from that ship, did you?"

Luckily, for once in his life, the skipper was quite sober, the effects of the drink he had consumed earlier, having worn off, a very rare occurrence to say the least.

"No matey; I haven't had a drink or seen one in twenty four hours, mores the pity, I could certainly do with one now, Are you offering to buy a shout then matey? Might be worth a feed of herring." he said, laughingly.

The customs officer didn't respond to the question, but appearances told him that the skipper was unusually sober. Not wanting to get into a heated argument the customs men succumbed to a bit of a micky take, knowing that to respond at present would ignite the calm situation.

We all continued for some time to take the micky out of the customs officers, knowing full well that they had nothing on us, and if a search was done, nothing of evidence could be found.

We set about boxing the rest of the herring that were lying on the canvas, and stacked the full boxes on the promenade ready for the old boatman to load on the cart and take to the yard, apart from a few boxes which were put aside for the public to buy direct, one of the beach helpers took up this task, as the money released from the sale of these couple of boxes was to be divided amongst the helpers, in a form of payment, a usual practice when a large catch was landed, besides it was cheaper than paying them a wage.

"Don't mind if we take a look-over the boat do you skipper? We had a report that you have some contraband aboard. Just to satisfy our records, that's all."

"You should be so lucky, we haven't had any such good fortune as that matey; you don't think I'd be standing here gasping for a drink if I'd got some spirits off that ship, do you?" He asked.

"All the same skipper, we would like to search your boat when you have finished boxing up, if that's alright with you?"

"No problem matey." the skipper replied. ."Let us get the boat clear first, come on Tom, set to here and get the fish out of the old girl's well. Snap lively now, these customs men are gasping for a drink. And his lordship don't want to be late for dinner now, does he?" the skipper sarcastically remarked again.

All hands hastily set to the task of relieving the hold of the boat from its remaining fish. The last box had hardly been lifted over the side, before the three customs men started clambering aboard. Footings came up, the engine case was removed and every thing in the fore and aft lockers was removed.

"Alright now matey's?" said the skipper with a big smile on his face." you've made a good job of your uniforms; they look quite colourful with the herring scales shining all over them." He said laughingly. ."No doubt they'll smell just as good in a couple of hours as well."

They certainly did look a pretty sight, covered from head to toe in herring slime and scales. But to rub salt into the wound the skipper insisted they put the boat back as they found it, every article, just as it was before they started to rip her up in their search. We couldn't help laughing, but put things back they did, it would have been the worst for them if they hadn't, and the skipper was known for his arrogant revenge, not a sight to see when angry.

Red faced and somewhat angry at their misfortune, the customs men disembarked the boat, and embarrassingly made their way up the beach, glittering in the sunlight like twinkling fairies.

"Cheerio matey's! Sorry we couldn't give you a drink, had we got some ourselves we would have more that obliged you, wont say no if you bring one back with you though." Shouted the skipper as the men proceeded to cross the promenade, amid the shouts and laughter of the onlookers. How embarrassing.

"We will catch you one of these days skipper, don't you worry, and we'll catch you, and then watch out." Came an angry reply, as they disappeared down King Street.

"That was a close shave Tom, nearly came a cropper that time, good job the old timer warned us, eh?"

The boxing was completed, with the fish that had already gone to my fathers' yard, and the boxes left on the promenade, we had made an excellent haul, which, if the weather didn't get any better in the next week or two, would keep us in comfort for a while.

Meanwhile, having a few excess boxes for sale, buyers had accumulated around, arguing amongst themselves, as to who was going to buy the catch.

"Look at them Tom, like little children, you'd think they had never seen a fish before, wouldn't you. If they are that eager to get their hands on our herring, then they can get eager to part with a good price. What do you recon Tom?"

"I recon you are about right there skipper do your best and get them going." I said

The skipper started to mingle with the arguing buyers, eying up the situation that was brewing amongst them.

"What's up men?" He bellowed, making himself heard above the noise. ."Not enough to go round?"

He moved towards a box and placing his hand deep within it, picked up a handful of herring.

"Nice sample aren't they? Should fetch a good penny on the open market. None been landed anywhere this week, has there?"

"Tell you all what I'll do!" he said. ."Tom and I haven't had a penny in our pockets for a couple of weeks now, all this wind and bad weather. Haven't been able to get afloat, if you see what I mean. If you are so desperate for them, I'll take a shilling a stone, not a penny less. Not a bad deal is it?"

He walked away and stood silently as the buyers threw curses at him,

"What are you doing skipper? They won't pay that price, it's too high. We'll get stuck with them." I remarked.

"Don't worry Tom, they'll pay the price, you will see."

Unmoved by his actions, the skipper moved back to the boat, leant against the after deck casually rolled a cigarette, lit it, and in a puff of smoke turned his head seaward in ignorance to the buyers behind him." They'll pay. ."He sniggered, they'll pay."

Within a few minutes the buyers had arranged between themselves to buy the remainder of the catch, at a shilling a stone as well. Although this was under great protest, and a lot of mumbling and disaprovement. They really had no choice in the matter; there wasn't any more herring along the coast to be had.

"Alright you robbing old bounder." One of the buyers shouted out. ."We'll take them all off your hands. Mind you, if there were more about you wouldn't get more than three pence a stone."

The payment and catch was sorted out between the skipper and the chief buyer, who paid for the herring on the spot in cash, and I had nothing to do with the selling, and looked on in wonder, still shaking my head at his brazen nerve in demanding such a high price. Still he achieved it and I shouldn't question the matter, after all, it was a bit more in my pocket, and after all the rough hard work we had done, we deserved every penny.

Whilst the loading and clearing up of the last fish was taking place, I stood gazing out to sea, in the direction of the ship that had unfortunately become stuck on the Goodwin Sands. She was still held fast, with towering pillars of water being thrown up high over her hull as the tremendous seas broke against her side. The masts had long since been carried away over her side. The tide had risen considerably by now, and with the conditions and heavy seas breaking on her, she should have been pounded to pieces, or at least been steadily thrown northwards with the wind, tide and sea pushing so hard against her hull, but she was holding firm, as if trying to struggle hard for survival, to grasp the last breath of life before the end came.

The first set of sail from one of the rescue boats that had launched from the beach was now just appearing out by the Deal bank buoy, heaving up and down in the heavy seas, disappearing out of sight every time she wallowed in one of the troughs, which was topped with a creamy white crest. Another hour or so and conditions on the beach would be too bad again for landing, and an attempt to do so would most probably end up in the boat being smashed to pieces on the beach, a risk not worth any salvage cargo. Other boats too, could now been seen heading back towards the shore.

"Hey skipper, the first galley's coming ashore from the wreck on the sands." I shouted as I clenched my eyes hard to try and see which boat she was.

"I see her Tom; we will have a stroll along and have a look, see what they have been up to out there. Shall we?"

With this we gathered ourselves together and walked steadily towards the southern side of the pier. By the short time it had taken us to reach the berth of this galley, she had beached and was already hove clear of the breaking surf. These boats were the fastest craft on the beach and turned a fair speed of knots under a full set of sail in a stiff breeze, the fastest of revenue cutters were given a haul for their troubles if trying to catch a galley, and as I know, no boat has yet ever overhauled the galley.

Enough hands were helping to haul the galley up the beach, so we stood at her moorings watching, until she was hauled up and made fast.

"Got something onboard her by the looks of it Tom, no survivors from the wreck though." the skippers. "Come on let's go and be nosey."

We walked across the beach to find out what had taken place out there on the Goodwin Sands. The skipper spoke to one of the galley's crew, whilst I kept carefully quiet and listened.

."Good morning mi old brancher, little bit of sea running out there this morning on the sands, isn't there?" The skipper asked. "How did you get on?"

"Ah! A bit wet skipper, not to bad though, we've been out in a lot worse. The ship's well aground on the bank though, she went ashore at the top of the tide last night. Apparently all the lights aboard her had been put out by the force of the wind and flying spray, they set light to a keg of oil to attract attention, but the poor fella's couldn't get it to flare, it just smoldered away on the deck." The crew member told the skipper

"We saw the smoke at daybreak." replied the skipper.

"Aye, they were lucky that she held together and didn't go to pieces, there's a huge sea running out there, she's taking a heck of a pounding."

"What have you got there mi old brancher?" asked the skipper nosily. "Anything any good?"

"Nothing much skipper, just a few chests of tea, couldn't leave it there now could we, wasn't worth coming home with an empty boat."

"What's happened to all her crew mi old brancher, where have they all gone, any survivors or have they all drowned?"

"No skipper, they are all safe thank God, one of the Luggers has managed to get them on board, we thought they'd be safer on a bigger boat; fourteen of them there are including a cat. It's a wonder they weren't all drowned though. Good job the tide was falling when she struck, otherwise they are all safe and alright."

The skipper glanced eagerly and anxiously again at the chests in the galley's well, something was going through his head and I wasn't sure if I was going to like it.

"How did you get on skipper, get any of them silver darlings last night? Didn't expect to see you afloat in those sea conditions How did it go?" asked the crew man.

"Oh, just a couple, not a lot doing." he replied.

Word had already gone around of our catch though, and these chaps already knew about our luck with the herrings, so there was no good in fooling them.

"Funny thing, you know skipper, we all heard that you came in gunwales under, had more than enough than your old boat could carry. Heard you have smuggled ashore some booty from one of them there ships too; not a bad night's work for you, eh?"

"I don't know who's given you that idea; we never got the chance to go along side any ships. Besides if we had got the opportunity to go alongside any ship in that weather we would be done for, we would have been swamped for sure with the weight of the fish we were carrying."

"Ah! So it's right then skipper, you did have a good catch, how did you get on then? We are sure to find out sooner or later, so you just as well tell us."

"Just a few me old brancher, just a few." he said calmly.

"What's just a few skipper? You know we had been told as soon as we hit the beach, some say that you had as many as thirty last; not bad eh?"

"Well news gets around fast on this beach, doesn't it? Can't get up in the morning before someone has told you what time you go to bed. Can you?"

"How did yer do then skipper?" he asked again.

"Ah well, we got around twenty last, damned hard work they were too in that sea and wind, nearly lost her a couple of times, the seas were running clean over her head. Damned hard work, we earn't every penny of it I might add."

A short period of silence fell over the air as the men of the galley gathered round the skipper to hear his tales.

"Didn't get drunk on that booty then?" one of the crew asked.

"What booty?" exclaimed the skipper?

"That booty you got from that there ship you went alongside, don't tell us you didn't go aboard her."

"We never got any booty did we Tom?" he said turning to me and looking for an answer to hold his claims.

"No skipper." I replied. "Didn't take a chance in that sea with the weight in our hold, she would have gone under."

"See mates; don't know where you heard that story from. We are not all that mad you know."

The men knew that the skipper had been along side the ship, it was obvious, they could see him from their position at the wreck, the same as we could see them, although he denied his activities I knew as well as them, that when night fell, they would be at his home buying a cheap bottle from him. He knew it as well.

"Anyway mi old brancher, what is the ship that's gone aground on sands carrying? Anything good?" asked the skipper.

"Almost as good as your herring catch skipper." one of the crew replied laughing. ."She's called the Fiona, a fine ship she was too, full of tea and coffee, with sides of salt beef."

The skipper's eyes lit up. ."What's her condition?" he asked.

"Not bad skipper, she's holding up on the fork spit, masts have gone, but her hull pretty solid, coffee is all spoiled though. If she gets through this tide without going to pieces she'll make some good salvage."

The customs officers had now arrived on the scene to take account of what was coming ashore in the rescue boats, and as was their custom, to impound any cargo, holding it over for the insurers, which would only pay a fraction of it's worth to the boatmen for saving it.

"Come on Tom." said the skipper." The smells getting ripe round here all of a sudden." he sarcastically said as he glanced one of the customs men directly in the eye. ."See you all later mates, usual place and time."

"Right oh!" came the reply from the galley's crew.

"Right Tom." said the skipper as we walked along the seafront back to our own berth. ."Right Tom, here's how it is. We are going out tonight on the tide if the weathers not too bad, we'll makes out we are going to shoot for herring, but we are going to get some of that salt beef from that wrecked ship out there, it should fetch a pretty penny you know. What do you say Tom?"

Staring closely at the ground and without hesitation I gave him my reply.

"Ok skipper I don't mind, could use a bit of beef myself, almost forgotten what it tastes like, anything for a penny or two. What about the customs, how are we going to avoid them seeing though?"

He was quick to answer this question, as many times in the past, fortune had come his way, and being one of the old boatmen, knew a trick or two as well as a few people in a high position.

"Don't you worry about a thing Tom, I'll get it all organized no one will know a thing; we'll just have a bad catch tonight. Come on now lets get the boat cleaned out and ready for tonight's tide."

The job of washing the scales from the boat's side and skilling the nets in ready for tonight was soon completed, with everything being made ready for tonight's launch.

"Good Tom, now I'm going to go and see about a couple of helpers for tonight that have barrows and can keep their mouths shut, also to sort out a buyer; you get that there brandy cleaned up, all the fish scales wiped off the bottles now, and get it to my house at seven tonight, you know what to do don't you? Be careful now, watch out those customs men, don't let them catch you, we don't want to lose it after all this trouble. See you at seven Tom."

"Right oh skipper, I know what to do, don't worry."

And with this we went our own individual ways, setting about the discrete tasks in hand.

****

CHAPTER FOUR

THE NIGHT HAUL

To avoid any kind of suspicion, I left the beach and went straight home, enjoyed a well cooked meal and a few hours rest.

Five o'clock came with darkness already setting in, it was time to move. Dressed in my sea gear, I made my way up to my father's house where the first boxes of herrings were sent, these were the ones in which I had hidden the brandy.

The gate was open, on entering, I saw the flickering of a candle coming from the store house where the herrings were prepared for curing, father was busy spitting* up the fish and hanging them on boxes to dry off, ready for smoking to make them into bloaters.

"Good evening son." He said to me as I strolled into the shed." Had a pretty good catch today didn't you?"

"Yes we did alright; did you find the goods in the boxes dad?" I asked.

"Yes son, the old chap sorted them out, as soon as he got down here, cleaned them up for you too, he's hid them in the herring hang under the sawdust. Took one for himself though, said the skipper told him he could have it."

Well the skipper didn't actually say he could have one but then we knew, as the old boatmen did, that he had us over a barrel so to say and he would have been given one anyway. I stayed for about an hour helping to spit herring with my father, talking about the night previous, and how events had taken place. The job of spitting up the herring done, and spits* hanging over the hang ready for the fire to be lit, I gathered up the bottles and placed them in a fish box on the front of a carrier bike, which I had borrowed from my father, and left for the skipper's house.

"Good night dad." I shouted as the gate slammed behind me.

As I came out into Brewer Street the wind hit me straight in the face, it had gone right round to the east'ard, blowing a fair stiff breeze as well. There'd be no going afloat tonight I thought to myself, it would be a heck of a job trying to launch into the teeth of an onshore breeze.

The skipper's house was soon reached, with the door opening almost before I had chance to lean the bike against the wall.

"Come in Tom hurry up before someone see's you." said the skipper eagerly.

I entered the door carrying the fish box full of bottles and kicked it shut behind me.

"Put them down there lad on the table, careful now, don't drop them."

I carefully placed the box on the table relieving my arms of the weight it contained. The room was dark and dank with only a small candle burning on the mantelpiece, a bit of fire glowed in the fireplace hardly alight for the want of a piece of wood, it was cozy though. The skipper's wife sat quietly in a rocking chair knitting, never once looking at what she was making. She had been doing this for so many years she could do it with her eyes shut, so the dark didn't affect her.

"Evening ma'am." I said as I sat in a chair on the other side of the fire." Not a very good night out there tonight, is it?"

A welcoming word came from under her bonnet and all was quiet again.

"The winds freshened up hard from the east'ard skipper." I said in a quiet voice." Doesn't look good for tonight."

I didn't get an answer, but before I had finished my last word, there was a knock at the door. The skipper opened it, poked his head out and looked around cautiously, checking that no-one except those whom he was expecting was about.

"Alright matey's come in, smartly now. Take a seat where you can." He said.

Half a dozen weather beaten men entered the room and found a seat where they could. It was the crew of the Lugger and the crew of the galley that we had spoken to earlier that day.

"Good evening skipper! Evening Tom." they all said as they sat down and made themselves at home.

"Right." Said the skipper. "Here's how it is."

"Hang on skipper." said the owner and skipper of the Lugger "do you think we should be launching tonight, there is a fair stiff breeze from the east'ard blowing up there now, and it might look a bit suspicious, everyone knows we don't catch herring on an easterly blow."

"Don't worry lads we've had worse haven't we? Here's how things are at the moment."

The skipper started to explain what was going to take place this evening; he had already arranged with these men earlier in the day as to what he wanted to do and all were well trusted men and good volunteers, the chance of a few pounds never went amiss by anyone, and if they could get the cargo ashore and sold without the customs finding out, all the better.

"We'll put a fleet of herring nets in each boat and catch a few herring. Then we'll go out to the ship on the sands and get some of that salt beef off her, fill each boat up with as much as we can."

"What about the tea skipper, are we taking some of that?" asked one of the men.

"It's up to you mates, but I've made arrangements with a buyer to take all the salt meat we can bring ashore, no questions asked, his wagons will be waiting, and they'll think its herring. We'll cover the boats with herring scales from the few we catch, make it look like we've had a good catch. You know you can catch a few of them on an easterly blow, just damned awkward hauling."

There was a slight pause before he spoke again.

"If the winds easterly, sure it's going to be a bit difficult launching, but don't worry I've got some lads coming up to help us, only cost a shilling a piece. You know them mates; they've helped us do this before."

"Right skipper." one man replied." What's the plan then on getting to the wreck?"

"Here mates, we launch as I said, get some herring, and then the three boats go out to the wreck. We'll use your galley to board her and ferry the cargo to and fro, the other two boats can anchor close. We'll get a good lea from the seas as the flood runs through. When we are all full we will come ashore, the boys will be ready for us, and start to unload while we winch up our craft. They'll load the wagons and they will get them away before we can get hauled up, ok!"

They all looked at the skipper." Someone's sure to know what's going on skipper when they see we haven't got much of a catch of herring aboard. What'll you tell them?" one of the crew men asked.

"Easy mate; Easterly wind! Shouldn't want any explaining, don't always catch many on an easterly do we?"

"Yes I suppose you are right skipper, can be pretty bad on an easterly."

"Right lads, we'll set out at midnight. Now to the other business on hand."

Everyone agreed on the nights plans and now the brandy was bought to the attention of the men who all wanted a bottle.

"Right I have got enough bottles for us all to have three each, if you don't want any I've got others who will pay a pretty penny for it. Best Napoleon it is; wasn't cheap either."

The brandy was taken out of the fish box and placed on the table; he glanced at me, and then looked at the bottles again.

"Alright Tom where is she? There's a bottle missing you aren't trying to rob your old skipper are you?"

"No skipper." I replied somewhat shakily." Father said the old boatman who brought the herring to his yard, told him that he could have one for his trouble he said that you told him it was alright."

The skipper looked back at me." Sorry Tom I forgot about him, best let that one go we had best let him keep his mouth shut! He did warn us of the customs men I suppose. Right here we are matey's, cost me one and six a bottle, it would cost you three shilling in the ale house, and not half as good. Who wants some?"

A deadly silence broke over the room, not a murmur from anyone. I knew what the skipper paid, the robbing old bounder. It was three hundred herring, nine stone at a shilling a stone selling price. Nine shillings, for a score or more bottles. These men knew it too; they knew the skipper all too well.

"Don't all shout at once will you? It's worth half a crown a bottle of anyone's money; I can sell it elsewhere you know!"

"You will only get one and six a bottle from the ale house skipper, and you know it yourself, and we know you didn't pay one and six a bottle for it." Said one of the men.

"Come on lads." said one of the other men." Times getting on, we've got to get afloat soon and we have the boats to get ready yet. Come on lets be going."

"Not so fast mates." said the skipper." Not so fast, you want a bottle or two don't you? I tell you what I'll do. I'll lose money and let you have it for one and six a bottle, but only because we are working together tonight mind you. How's that strike you all."

"To please you skipper." said one of the boatmen." Just to please you, we'll buy them all. But only to keep you from getting drunk on it."

After a slight pause the skipper answered." It's a deal mates; there it is, help yourselves. Here Tom! Here's a bottle for you, no charge. And don't say your skippers mean!"

The bottles of brandy were divided out amongst the men. I knew that when a bottle was given to me that this would be my share of the booty, not having a penny more from the sale, it's happened before. All satisfied we left the skippers house and went our own ways

"See you at midnight mates. Don't forget we'll meet at the wreck of the ship."

The door of the house slammed shut behind them." Good that's that lot gone Tom, here there's five shilling for you."

I was overwhelmed with his generosity; he'd never given me a penny before. Quickly I grabbed it and stowed it in my pocket.

"Thanks skipper its good of you."

"That's alright Tom you earned it last night, besides you are a damn good hand, right, you get up the beach and get the boat ready, and I'll be up shortly. I've got to go and see a man about tonight. I won't be long, we are going to earn a good bit tonight Tom."

Leaving the house, I took my money and my bottle home, and then proceeded up to the beach.

The wind was blowing almost a gale from the east with the tide almost up. The moon was covered with a blanket of thick cloud, and where the wind had changed from the sou'west to the east'ard, the swell had dropped away. It would be a few hours yet before the seas started running in heavily from an easterly direction. Launching shouldn't be too difficult, let's hope the moon stays hidden, as conditions were ideal for the task in hand.

I set about getting the boat ready to launch straight away, there wasn't a lot to prepare. A couple of extra nets were stowed on board, the woods greased and laid, and the main mast and sail shipped aboard, there'd be no noise tonight. The skipper wasn't long in arriving; he was dressed in his black oilskins and leather thigh boots.

"How are you getting on Tom, nearly ready?"

."Aye skipper, she's all ready to go."

The skipper glanced along the beach straining his eyes in the dark to see if he could see the other two boats that were to join us this night.

"Seen anything of the others yet Tom?" he asked as he glanced through the darkness in the direction to where the other boats were berthed.

"The galley punts gone clear of the pier head about half hour ago, haven't seen the Lugger launch yet."

"Well I can't see the Luggers mast on the beach, she must be off there." replied the skipper. ."Come on Tom lets get afloat, not much sea running at the present, should be pretty easy to beat out against this wind tonight."

As we were about to launch four young lads appeared on the scene.

"Here we are skipper." one of them gasped as he tried to get his breath, "we've run all the way along the beach to here, the Luggers just gone afloat, do you want a hand?"

These were the lads that the skipper had engaged for the night to unload the cargoes should everything go to plan.

"Come on then boys." he quietly whispered." Get on those lower woods, not too much noise now. You get on that slip chain son and when I say so, you let her go ok? You all know what to do when the boats come in don't you?"

"Yes skipper we do, don't worry about a thing, we will be here waiting."

"Right Tom lets hoist the mizzen and jib."

I hoisted the jib whilst the skipper hoisted the mizzen.

"Are you ready with the main halyard as soon as we strike the breakers Tom?"

"Aye skipper I'm ready." I replied.

He looked around at the boys then at me and then a glance at the sea.

"She's going to run to the south'ard as she leaves the bank lads, so get ready with those lower woods. Let go! The order came as suddenly to them as it did to me.

The slip chain released, the boat rushed towards the sea, clearing the beach as she went over the fall*. Crash, she came down like a towering tree, rushing over the woods which were quickly thrust beneath her, crunching and grinding her way into the sea. With a large bang and a wall of spray she lifted to the demands of the sea, swinging round to the sou'east as soon as there was enough water under her keel to float her, with the strong wind catching every bit of canvas we were offering it.

"Get the mainsail up Tom, quickly now before we blow back on to the beach."

I struggled quickly to hoist the mainsail while the skipper steered her out away from the beach. As the sail was made fast and the sheets tightened, she listed over further and further, quickly gathering speed seaward. A few hundred yards out and we changed tack, heading nor'east, out beyond the pier head. With a flood tide and easterly wind, we soon reached up off Sandown Castle, we tacked again to the sou'east, this would now give us a course due south, allowing for the flow of the tide.

On reaching the pier head and preparing to shoot a couple of herring nets we were surprised by the galley.

"Ahoy there skipper." came a voice from within the galley" We're coming along side."

"Wonder what they are up to Tom, something wrong?"

"Don't know skipper, look out here they are."

As I said this, the galley came along side, both boats still under sail and making way through the water.

"Look skipper we shot two nets, sea must be full of herring, we've got over a thousand of them. Don't shoot yours; here take some of these it will save us a great deal of time."

The lads in the galley started throwing herring in all directions at us.

"Alright skipper! Should do the trick eh? See you at the wreck."

With this they hauled clear of us, heading toward the fork spit where the wreck of the Fiona struck last night. We couldn't catch them if we tried. Too fast, those galleys.

"Come on Tom." the skipper shouted." Rub the scales around the boat and make it look good."

He tightened in on the sheets, altered our heading toward the fork and rapidly the boat healed over to the command, gathering speed all the time.

"Twenty minutes and we'll be there Tom. Have a rest you'll need it."

I settled back into the bows with my head covered, avoiding the constant stream of spray that was coming over her gunwales, taking advantage of the short period of rest available. For sure enough, it was going to be heavy going, running beef sides from the wreck to the boats, especially in this wind.

We soon reached the wreck and anchoring just to the west of her made out the shape of the Lugger ahead of us.

"Ahoy there in the Lugger everything ready?" shouted the skipper.

"Aye skipper we're ready." came the reply.
The galley punt came along side." Are you fit skipper?" shouted a voice." Come on jump in."

And with this the skipper jumped aboard the galley.

There were five in her now; one had been taken off the Lugger. Three of them would go on board the wreck and load the galley, then two would sail her to and fro to our boat and the Lugger, each time with a load of cargo.

"Take care Tom, don't let her drift away now." came the last cry from the skipper as the galley vanished into the darkness and out of sight.

The wait seemed forever, with the seas slowly getting bigger and heavier, when suddenly there was a shout, breaking the constant drone of the sea and the wind.

"Ahoy there Tom; we are coming alongside."

It was the galley, she was back. ."We've taken two loads to the Lugger, thought you could do with some." he shouted.

She came alongside dropping her mainsail at the same time, the crew immediately throwing wrapped halves of beef over the gunwales into my boat.

"Get them stowed well Tom, we'll be back shortly with another load."

With this the galley hoisted her sail and vanished once more into the dark. I carefully stowed the beef in the boat's hold, but before I finished the task they were back with another load. Three of the men had been left aboard the wreck to get the cargo out, making it quicker to transport.

"Another load Tom, how are you doing? We are going to load the Lugger now so that she can get ashore and get rid of her lot first."

The beef sides once more were thrown over the gunwales into my boat, and quickly they disappeared into the night again. Some half hour passed before they returned with another load.

"We've got another load for you Tom, the Luggers gone ashore full." shouted the skipper.

"We've got to get back quick, the wrecks starting to shift with the sea; she'll be breaking up soon if we don't get a move on. Back in a bit."

Again they disappeared and left me to stow the cargo. I'd just finished when the galley came alongside once more.

"All clear Tom." the skipper shouted as he jumped aboard, as the galley passed alongside. ."See you ashore mates, make haste now."

The galley left with astonishing speed and within seconds was gone out of sight.

"The wreck's just about done now Tom, she's breaking up fast with this wind, shouldn't be surprised if she isn't there in the morning, scary on her too. Come on then, lets get the anchor weighed, the others will be unloaded and gone home before we get ashore if we don't look sharp."

We both pulled as hard as we could on the anchor cable, slowly bringing the anchor up to the boat's side, and then bringing it inboard, set the sails on half reef and made full speed for the shore. Turning the boat's head before the wind and sea, she thrust foreword with almost unstoppable speed. Daylight was but three hours away, so we had to get ashore and cleared as quickly as possible. In the distance the twinkering of a faint light could be made out, barely visible through the spray and haze.

"Head for the light Tom." shouted the skipper.

He had always given me the privilege of taking the helm for the run shoreward, quite an easy task in this wind. She fled before the easterly wind like an albatross; rushing ever faster on the swells as they ran before us, lifting us by the stern and throwing us before them. With the weight of the meat aboard she didn't even roll but laid steady, she always was a good boat in a bit of sea when loaded.

The skipper settled back on the fore thwart, relaxing for ten minutes, a well earned break too I should have thought, it must have been hard work on the wreck unloading lumps of meat, some of them weighing a hundredweight each.

"Give me a shout when we reach the pier head Tom, I'm going to have a minute with my eyes shut you know!"

"Alright skipper, shouldn't be long though at this rate."

The tide was almost slack now and would have fallen well below the high water bank, thus making beaching pretty easy. The swells were small and sharp, not giving any threat of filling us when we beached; it would be the next high water when the swells would be at their worst as it took twenty four hours to build up after strong easterlies. It wasn't long; the pier head came looming up on our bows

"We's here skipper, the pier heads on our bows."

"Right Tom I'll take the helm now."

Without another word he clambered aft and took the tiller.

"Get the chain reeved Tom; I'm going to run under full sail, try to beach her high. Hope those lads are waiting and ready."

Climbing over the cargo, I grabbed hold of the foremast, quickly reeved the chain and made ready to beach. Two figures were seen on the beach at the waters edge waving us in.

"The lads are there skipper, all's ready."

With this we came hard ashore and with such speed she grinded her way almost clear of the water's edge. Quickly the lads hooked her onto the winch wire, whilst the skipper and I lowered the sails.

She started moving, the weight was on the winch wire and she was gradually going up the beach. That meant the other lads had finished their work with the Lugger and galley.

"Alright boys!" exclaimed the skipper." How has the work gone with the other boats, any trouble?"

One of the lads breathlessly turned to the skipper and answered.

"No skipper everything's alright, they have been unloaded and the crews and wagons are gone, no one is about yet. Wagons are waiting topside for your lot skipper."

"Good boys lets get her up then."

With rapid speed she raised the fall and came to rest on her stocks, the other two boys securing the winch and rushing to the boats side.

"Right boys get her unloaded, we'll help you, never mind the boat lets get rid of the cargo and carts."

It didn't take but a short while for us all to unload the cargo, with six of us working away, and in no time the carts were rolling down King Street loaded with their unsuspecting goods.

"Nice work boys, you've earn't your money tonight. Did the Lugger get ashore on top of the tide?"

"She did skipper, had eight cart loads in her too, we got her unloaded in less than half hour and all the carts away."

"Good boys, now here's what you have to do."

"Tom and I are going to disappear home for a couple of hours rest, you boys get the nets out of her and then go and get the nets out of the galley. Then you all can have the fish from both boats and sell them bit of a bonus you might say. I'll give you your wages in the morning. Alright? Tom and I will be back here at nine o'clock sharp. But mind you keep your mouths shut or else."

"Yes skipper." they all shouted as they scrambled to relieve the boat of its catch and nets.

."Bit of extra money always worked a wonder Tom didn't it? Come on let's go home."

He leant over the boat and pulled half a side of beef out, throwing it over his shoulders.

"Didn't think I was going without after all that work did you Tom? Need a feed don't we? I'll cut you a lump off; don't you worry."

We started walking down Market Street and towards our houses. The skipper explained how the Lugger having beached at high tide would not be suspected of even being afloat, as the tide would have washed away all evidence of launching. It would have given the game away if they found out she'd been off, that's why she was loaded first and sent ashore.

The galley and our boat had left beach marks of our landing below the fall, as the tide had dropped when we had landed, showing all that we had been afloat, but that didn't matter. We had a catch of herring aboard to prove our goings on and the lads to say they helped us shake out. A good disguise as far as anyone would suspect we had a bad catch of herring because of the easterly wind, that wasn't unusual anyway.

"Good night Tom, see you at nine." Said the skipper, as we came to St. George's alley. ."Don't be late now!" with that we both parted and went our own ways.

Where the meat went and who had purchased it no one knew except the skipper, but we could all be sure in this deal with the buyers, everyone would be treated fairly and squarely, as further supplies wouldn't be coming if someone was undercut. We had many times before worked the flanker on a wreck, leaving it short of cargo, and as yet, never been found out although it had been close at times. Daylight was now on the horizon, so a quick hot drink and a sit down for an hour was all I was going to get this morning.

At half past eight I dressed for the weather and left my house, the wind was still blowing hard from the east, and a cold damp mist covered everything in a wet film.

Arriving back up the beach, I saw a group of men in the covering seats talking to each other. It was the skipper and the crews of the other boats, no harm in this I thought, in bad weather the boatmen always gathered to view the sea on the off chance of a Hubble. (That's Deal language for a rescue or a bit of salvage)

"Good morning skipper, morning all." I said as I pushed my way into the group of boatmen." How's it going?"

"The lads have sold all the herring but the best news is, that the wreck of the Fiona out there on the spit has gone, she's broke up and gone Tom." Said the skipper.

There was quietness, they all knew too well that during the night we had made a good haul and been unsuspected, but now the wreck had gone no one would even suspect that us, or any other boat, had been out to her. This was the best thing that could have happened.

Not much else to do that day, we just pottered around doing odd jobs, a little bit of mending, scrubbing down and a general tidy up. The boys that had helped during the night came wandering along late that afternoon, looking for their money, of course.

"Hello skipper, how are you going?" one of the boys shouted as he approached us.

."Might have expected it to be you lot." Harry groaned." What's up spent our herring money already eh?"

The four boys gathered around the skipper wearily looking him up and down.

"Well skipper it's not that we don't trust you, but you do have a notion to forget things after a day or so, don't' you? Especially money!"

"Ah you lads are all the same, as if the old skipper would rob you all of a shilling, you must have earn't a few shilling on those herring I gave you last night. 'Wasn't that enough then, eh?"

"Aye skipper, but you did promise us a shilling each to turn out last night; didn't you? Besides, without our help you would never have got the boats ashore and the goods away so quick. Still, we can always tell the customs men what went off if you like, they would be more than pleased to know."

"Alright! Alright, I'll give you a shilling each out of my own pocket, here you are, now be off with you, robbing little scoundrels."

"Thanks skipper, if you need any more work done you know where to find us. Any time of the day or night."

Thrusting the money into their pockets, the boys scampered away. The skipper, red faced from having to part with a few bob, began muttering beneath his breath disgruntingly.

"Well you did promise them a shilling apiece skipper." I said to him. ."Didn't you?"

"Aye Tom, I recon I did, still they did do a pretty good job didn't they? Well! It's no good standing here in this easterly gale complaining, and getting wet in the spray, we just as well go and have a pint or two of ale. Are you coming Tom? He replied.

With this we both set a course for The Three Compasses Inn, not far away at the top of Coppin Street.

The Doors of the inn were firmly shut, and required a strong shove to open them; being on the seafront the inn was wide open to the winds in an easterly direction. The landlord had placed some old clothes along the bottom of the door to stop the rushing onslaught of the cold easterly wind gaining access, but even this couldn't completely stop the keenest of draughts entering the room, twisting round all the corners and cutting a cold edge on everyone's feet.

Within the inn seated around the log fire which was flickering in the far corner, were some of the older boatmen, with a few of the crews from the boats that were engaged with us last night on the Goodwins, taking off the salt beef.

"Hello skipper." one of the boatmen shouted across the room as we came in." What's your poison?" By this he meant what would you like to drink, as he was offering to buy.

"The usual old fella and the same for Tom thanks."

We wandered over to the fire and sat at the table with the other members of last nights working crews, talking about recent events and supping a few glasses of ale. The prospects of a hovel or wreck on the inner part of the Goodwin Sands had almost been blown away; as not much shipping attempted to sail along the inside edge in an easterly blow for fear of being driven ashore if something happened to go wrong. Most stayed well out to seaward of the sands.

Merrily singing away and enjoying our ale, we were suddenly disturbed by a rush of cold wind coming through the side door of the Inn as it was flung wide open to the elements. Entering the doorway was a tall well dressed gentleman, a right posh one as well. Slamming the door hard behind him as he entered and looking around at us, he asked in a low posh voice.

"Good day my dear fellows, has anyone here seen the chap called, skipper about?"

Moving to the bar he ordered a large brandy and sat on one of the tall bar seats, glancing around the room of the inn, obviously he was unaccustomed to sitting in such a place as this, and was more used to the posh city type inns with their comfort and cleanliness.

"Here I am Sir!" the skipper suddenly piped up. ."What would you be looking for me for, something the matter is there?"

"I have a business proposition to make to you skipper if you are interested, come and join me for a minute and I'll discuss it with you. Barman!" he shouted. ."Fetch this good fellow another drink."

The two men sat at the other end of the room away from listening ears and peering eyes. It was obvious to me by the way the skipper reacted to this gentleman, that he had made his acquaintance before and knew him quite well.

Something very fishy was going on here, a package was passed over the table from the gentleman to the skipper, picking it up the skipper took off his hat, placed it inside and put his hat back on his head again. What was he up to I wondered?

"Thank you sir, everything was to your satisfaction was it; no problems at all?" The skipper asked the gentleman, making sure all about him could now hear the conversation.

"Yes skipper, that was a good drop of stuff you had there, any time you come across some more you know where to come to dispose of it, you are always welcome."

The gentleman finished his brandy, bade the skipper a good day and left the inn, once again letting in a rush of bitter cold air as he opened the door to depart. Returning back at our table and taking his place up in his chair again, the skipper sipped gently at his drink, staring at us through the top of his cap, waiting for one of us to ask him what was going on, he knew we were eager to find out.

"Who was that posh gentleman skipper?" I asked first, breaking the silence.

"Never you mind Tom, doesn't matter who that was or what his business was about."

The skipper took off his hat and removed the brown parcel from within it, placed the parcel on the table and proceeded slowly to unwrap it. We were all amazed to see the contents, a pretty sight on a cold day like this.

"There matey's, look at that, nice little gift isn't it?" Before us all lay a bundle of one pound notes, tied neatly with an expensive piece of red ribbon.

"That's what the gentleman bought me matey's, our pay for the nights work on relieving that ship of her cargo, doesn't matter who he is, it's best if you don't know."

Taking hold of the pile of notes the skipper started to share it out into equal lots for the men that had been involved in the salving of the salt beef last night, this also included a share for each boat as well, as most boats, although manned by a good crew, had an owner that lived away from the town and very rarely came to visit, except on the odd occasion to draw some money for use of the boat. This was the boat's share.

"There we are mates, nine pounds each, not a bad wage for a quick nights work was it?"

We took our share of the money and quickly thrust it into our pockets, in case someone should become inquisitive as to where it had all come from, it was obvious that the small catch of herring never made this sort of money, besides we had given them to the lads that helped us.

"Thanks skipper," we all said, "We could do with another haul like that; it would keep a stew going on our stoves for quite some time."

"Not being funny skipper." I said in a low tone voice. "But I noticed that there's about seven and sixpence still on the table unaccounted for. Did you have a use for this, or is there another crew member not here that we don't know about?"

"Ah! So you think I'm trying to fiddle you do you Tom?" he exclaimed. ."There's not enough there really to share out in that small change, I was going to put it over the bar so you could all have a drink with it; Ah! Not trusted." he angrily said.   ."Here! You take it, put it over the bar, and I hope you choke yourself on it."

"I didn't mean it like that skipper its just that I wondered what it was for, thanks anyway."

With this I got up and gave the money to the barman, this would give us a few free beers during the week when things were a bit hard.

The money we received from the smuggling had paid off well, there was more than enough to live on for several weeks to come, and I still had my wages from the herring catch to come yet as well. Should the weather prevail for much longer I certainly would have no worries.

"Well!" One of the boatmen said! ."I'm off now, see you all in the morning, we wont be going anywhere tonight with this wind blowing."

"Aye, I'm away also." Said another boatman as he rose from his seat.

"I recon we have all done here for the day lads don't you?" said the skipper as he stood up and moved towards the door, followed closely by each and every one of us.

Following the skipper across the seafront and back onto the beach again, we both took a hard glimpse back out onto the sea, getting our faces stung by the spray that was driving hard shoreward from the force of easterly the wind.

"Well Tom, there's nothing doing out there this evening, not many sails about, cant say as I blame them, it's a rough old night." The skipper said as he pulled his cap further over his eyes to stop the spray stinging his face.

"Wait a minute Tom, what's that out there close by the Brake Lightship, can you see it?"

I stared seaward towards the Brake Lightship, which lay about three miles off shore to the nor'east, clenching my eyes to rid them of the salt water that was driving into my face. Sure enough I could make out the cloudy shape of a set of masts and a blur of a hull, just visible in the fading light and spray from the broken sea.

"It looks like a ship of some kind skipper, can't quite make her out with all this spray coming over me."

The skipper put his hand to his head, looking out to sea in the direction of the Brake Lightship, and then started to make his way to the beach hut which was situated a few yards away, gathering his telescope; he focused it in the direction of the masts, silently saying nothing, just staring out to sea.

"Here, have a look Tom, see what you recon."

I took the telescope from the skipper, put it towards my eye and swung around in the direction of the ship. Amazed, I saw a large full rigged ship running heavily with all canvas set before the wind, she was taking a bad course on her passage through the narrow channel of the Gull stream, a cut in the Goodwin Sands by which shipping gained a route to the north sea. On her deck could be made out something we all knew only too well.

****

Chapter Five

The Wreck of the Frederick

We could just make out a flare burning on the ship's deck as she rapidly run the gauntlet between the banks of the Goodwin Sands and the banks of the Brake, not a very nice place to be in conditions like this. Heavy seas were crashing down all around her and broken water was being flung high in the air, aided by the strong wind.

"Let me have another look Tom." Said the skipper as he snatched the telescope from my hands and thrust it against his left eye.

"Sure enough Tom, she's burning a distress flare, and with the heading she's on she won't clear the Brake sands. Go and get the others Tom, we had better get ready for a launch."

As the skipper said this we heard a loud boom come from the direction of the Brake Lightship. The lightships had cannon on board and used these to warn vessels of any danger they might be running into. Boom! Another report came from the Brake lightship, but the sailing vessel fast approaching the Brake didn't alter course.

"Doesn't look good Tom; go get the others, quick now."

Another boom sounded as I started to run across the road, the ships in trouble now I thought to myself as I made all haste to the other boatmen's houses. Each house in turn called at and the message left, I made my way back up to the beach where the skipper was still standing, watching the ship through his telescope in the fast fading light.

"Did you tell them all Tom?"

"Yes skipper, they are all on their way here, shouldn't be long."

"Good Tom, we'll get two of our boats to launch to the ship, there should be enough hands altogether to get us afloat. It won't be easy in this wind and sea, but we can't let the ship sink without attempting to give assistance, can we?"

Many boatmen had by now reached the seafront and were standing alongside the skipper discussing the situation, when we witnessed what we expected but what we didn't want to happen. The gun on the Brake lightship was now firing constantly, calling us on the shore to the scene, suddenly in a huge cloud of spray we saw the ship's bows lift high in the air, only to fall again amid a huge sea, she rolled onto her starboard beam and capsized, seas were now breaking over her full length.

"Quick mates get a couple of boats away, she will go to pieces in no time in this sea, poor souls won't stand a chance." said the skipper.

Two of the largest Luggers were made ready for launching, each boatman knowing the job which had to be done, woods were laid whilst others greased them, oilskins were put on and the crews of the two boats climbed aboard, the skipper and I securing a place in one of them.

The tide was low, so there was some way to travel down the beach before gaining the sea, in one way this was ideal as launching was always easier at low tide, the seas never had the huge verosity of the high water seas.

More boatmen arrived on the beach and were busily getting other boats ready for launching, hoping for a spot of salvage on the cargo if it was valuable enough. Beach hands were plentiful as well, which was a blessing as we needed all the help possible for launching, although most had only come up to earn a few pounds from any cargo that might be saved from the stricken ship.

Within no time our boat had been made ready, and we were now prepared for the launch, this was a privilege given to the most skilled boatman on board, which happened to be the skipper. He would take the helm and give the shout to let go.

"Everything ready lads?" the skipper shouted out over the beam as he stared seawards.

"Yes." came a load reply." Ready when you are skipper."

The skipper set his eyes seawards to the north, watching every wave as it came towards the shore and broke in a furious pile of spray, closely he studied the waves to get their pattern as they ran in, timing had to be perfect, allowing for the time it took

the Lugger to run down the beach and hit the sea, if the wrong wave came in as she hit, then disaster could happen, we could be knocked back ashore and have the Lugger destroyed as she lay helpless in the surf. Then suddenly he bellowed out.
"Let Go!"

The loud report of the skipper's voice broke the roar of the wind and the crashing waves on the foreshore.

Within seconds the slip chain had been released allowing the Lugger to move from her berth. Steadily she picked up speed as she slid over the greasy woods, faster and faster she went onward to the sea, less than a minute had passed when at speed faster than a dog could run, she left the last wood at the water's edge and buried her head into an oncoming sea. A mighty towering pillar of white water and foam engulfed her as she struck her way seawards, sails were rapidly hoisted and took the force of the wind, bellowing them out over the starboard side, over she heeled taking in another huge sea as she tried to pull clear of the threatening surf, a sudden calm came upon her and no sooner had she recovered from the last breaker than she gathered way and sped off seaward, throwing spray high into the air as the broken seas tore at her bows.

Carrying every bit of canvas we dared to give her in the conditions we cleared the pier head in record time, the helm was put over onto the port tack, sheets tightened in and course set for the Break lightship.

Some three quarters of an hour later we glimpsed the light of the Brake lightship, just about visible through the spray which constantly covered us from fore to aft. Closely behind us we could just make out the outlines of two other boats that had managed to launch from the beach.

During the passage to the Brake sands all sight of the ship had been lost, so the skipper made a course for where he thought the ship would be if she had struck bottom, allowing for the wind and tide which were both running in the same direction. Typical of an easterly wind, was the mist, which had thickened slowly into a thin fog, making the task of finding the ship in the dark even more hazardous.

"We are going to have to haul up on the lightship mates, we can hail her and get directions as to where the ship is lying." shouted the skipper over the howling wind.

The lightship could be seen quite clearly to our seaward side, its light becoming brighter as we sped on and out.

"Change tack mates, hurry up, get her round to starboard," he shouted as he forced the tiller over to port. The huge mainsail came crashing to the deck and was quickly reset and hoisted up again on the other side of the mast. Luggers carry a dipping lug sail, which meant they had to lower sail then unhook it and re-hoist it on the other side of the mast, otherwise the boat would capsize. Once again she heeled over to the pull of the sail, and on towards the lightship a few hundred yards away.

Quickly we hauled up under the lightship's stern and slackened off the sheets just enough to keep her steady.

"Where away lies the ship in distress mates, can you see her?" cried the skipper to the lightship crew.

A rugged built red faced man dressed in bright yellow oilskins was leaning over the rail of the lightship, watching us as we struggled to maneuver alongside in the awful sea conditions.

"Last we saw of her she was about a quarter of a mile to the north of us mate, looked like she was hard and fast aground, watched her for quite a while until the lights went out on her. Doesn't look too good mate, that's all I can tell you."

"Thanks old fella." Shouted the skipper as he turned the helm out towards the north, Sheets hauled taught and healing over to port , we began beating up against the tide and wind to the last seen position of the vessel in distress.

All eyes now scanned the horizon in the hopes of glimpsing a mast and sail or the outline of a ship's hull, she was a big ship so it shouldn't be hard to pick her up. All of a sudden one of our crew shouted out.

"There she is skipper," he bellowed."Right ahead of us, over there."

A huge sea hit our bows at that moment, knocking the poor fellow off his feet and to the deck below, soaking him from top to toe. Cursing and swearing he gained his foothold again and took up his watch in the bow.

The skipper stared intensely into the blackness of the night, straining to try and pick out the silhouette of the ship's shape against the heaving spray.

."There she is." he shouted. ."Fifty yards ahead on our bows, couldn't have struck the ground in a worse place."

Spray was rising high over her decks as the huge seas buffeted against her side, her masts had been carried away, leaving broken stubs in their place, snapped off like pieces of firewood. Smoke was blowing over her starboard side coming from a barrel on deck, they had tried to keep a distress fire burning on deck but on hitting the ground and healing over, this was immediately put out just leaving a few smoldering rags. No wonder we couldn't see her.

The vessel had struck the bottom and was firmly aground on the sandbank, every sea that came in and hit her flung tons of white bitter cold spray high up over her decks. With the tide running south at a good four knots and a strong following wind, conditions would only get worse, the boiling and fierceness of the sea as it ran over the Brake sands was more than we expected, this was going to be a dangerous task, getting alongside the wreck in these conditions, but knowing the skipper, he would do it.

As the tide was on the turn we had no choice, more water under the ship's keel meant that she would start lifting and pounding on the sand bank, combined with the force of the sea crashing down on her deck it wouldn't be long before she went to pieces, I've seen this happen so many times before.

Slowly the skipper fetched up on her leeward side, giving us a bit of shelter from the wind and sea, the ship was heeling over badly to starboard and rolling heavily as she was buffeted by the huge seas continually breaking on her port side, a fine ship she was, looked like a British merchantman, bigger than the usual merchant that came this way, not very old either, and with a name like ."Frederick." she must be British.

"Make ready lad." Came a shout from the skipper as we slid alongside the Frederick. "Grab a hold of those ropes hanging over her side; quickly now."

His voice momentarily disappeared in a mumbling gurgle as a huge sea rushed across the Frederick's deck and came crashing down upon us, giving the skipper a mouthful of fresh salt water.

Frantically we set about securing our Lugger to the side of the Frederick, every sea that came over the gunwales threatened to fill us with water and overwhelm us, pumps and buckets were manned to keep the water level as low as possible, an arduous task as we were filling almost as quickly as we were pumping out.

"This is going to have to be quick matey." shouted the skipper. ."We can't stay alongside her too long, it's too dangerous, besides she'll start to break up as the tide makes. Tom! Take two lads with you and get aboard."

The Frederick was well over on her starboard beam by now; rigging and spars were lying all around her still attached by their ropes. I could make out the shadow of some figures lashed to the deck housing up foreword, constantly being smothered in water as every wave became more and more forceful.

Climbing over her rail and gripping on to one of the numerous ropes lying along her side, we made our way up forward to where the poor souls were tied.

By now another Deal boat had arrived on the scene, a galley, pulling up fast and two of her men jumping into the hanging rigging, and then as quickly as she came she disappeared up ahead of the wreck. This was a common way of boarding, to leave some men on board then shoot ahead of the wreck and anchor, slowly paying out cable until the galley fell back and laid alongside,

Several times we were knocked almost over the side whilst trying to make our way aft, and now we were joined by the other two boatmen.

"Are you alright Tom?" Shouted one of the boatmen." what's the position?"

"Up here mates, there's some poor fellows tied to the fore deck house, we are going to try and get them off." I replied.

Making our way further forward and getting pounded by the sea we finally reached the deck house, The Frederick was starting to heave in the swells, her hull ripping and tearing, with loud reports as her timbers started to break under the strain.

"Come on old fella; let's get you out of here." I said to the first chap that I came across who was secured to the deck house. As I untied him he thanked me and asked that I put priority in saving the others.

"That's not a problem old fella! Are you up to giving me a hand for a bit, you look quite done in, no problem if you're not I'll get you back to the boat?"

"That's not a problem laddie; I've plenty of strength left, let's get these other poor souls off and into the boat then."

Gasping heavily and almost exhausted, he gave me a hand to unlash the other poor souls that were almost done in by the sea and cold.

"Use this rope to tie them together old fella, put it round their waists, just in case a heavy sea should come and wash them over board., That's it old fella, come on follow me everyone."

Carefully and steadily we all made our way along the sloping deck of the Frederick, holding on to anything that was available as the seas now rocked and pounded her heavier than ever.

"There she is, there's our boat," I shouted as I hailed the boat and waved my arms rapidly in the air.

The Skipper was anxiously awaiting our arrival, and skillfully hauled the boat alongside the Frederick, each wave almost smashing her to pieces as she was thrown against the side of the wreck.

."Hurry up my friends; lets get you off this wreck before she goes to pieces beneath us."

Forcing my way towards the rail I managed to grab the hauling rope the skipper had thrown me, made it fast and stared down into the Lugger which was being tossed about like a piece of driftwood.

"Thank heavens you are safe Tom, I was beginning to get worried, nearly sent some lads aboard to find you. I can't see a damn thing in this spray and blackness now. Come on lad; let's get you all aboard, hurry now."

He grabbed the first man's arm and pulled him into the Lugger, then the second and the third. After a couple of minutes all ten of the survivors were safely aboard the Lugger, and then I took an almighty jump and landed almost on top of the skipper.

"You alright Tom?" he asked as I stumbled to my feet.

"Aye skipper, lets get out of here."

We fended the Lugger off from the side of the wreck, when in the silhouette of the sky more people could be seen on her stern, frantically waving and running up and down.

"What about those other poor souls' skipper, look there's still some aboard her." I shouted.

."Don't worry Tom, there's other boats here, one has a crew aboard just astern of us I'm sure they'll rescue the poor blighters. More than we dare do to attempt another boarding, besides these poor fellows are just about done by and need to be taken ashore as soon as possible."

The survivors that we had picked up were huddled into the centre of the Lugger and given some blankets to wrap up in, not much help, but at least it would keep the biting wind off them so they didn't freeze to death.

As the anchor came inboard, sail was set and heeling over, the Lugger pulled clear of the stricken vessel. We could just about see the outline of a couple of large Deal Luggers hulls bobbing up and down astern of the wreck. I had been too busy saving myself and these other poor ten souls than to notice what was going on around me.

"Looks bad skipper." I said as I sat down on the after deck alongside the skipper who was fighting with the helm." This sea keeps running like it is and hopes of the wreck surviving much longer don't look very good, do they."

I turned to the first man that I had rescued as he was close by me, in the hopes of trying to find out what exactly had happened on board the Frederick, how she came to get in a distressed position eventually going aground. It turned out that she was carrying passengers to Australia when she was blown onto the northern tip of the Goodwins, striking the bottom hard, which sprung open part of her bows. Her skipper decided to take a chance in running before the wind directly towards the shore of Deal, where he thought he might beach the ship and be able to save all the souls onboard, but the water was coming in through the bow too fast, and filling fast she settled heavier into the water, making her wallow bad until all steering was lost.

The pumps were manned and working as fast as the crew could go, but it was hopeless, she was sinking lower and lower into the water, with all her canvas set, she flew rapidly before the wind and sea, then the worst happened, she struck the bottom with an awful grinding crash, the timbers almost being ripped from within her hull, she ran on again grinding and tearing along the sea bed, then a sudden stop. She heeled over heavily taking a couple of huge seas aboard at the same time, then one after the other her masts collapsed overboard and were carried away. We hadn't a chance then of saving her. A barrel was set alight on the deck, but no sooner had this been lit than a sea swamped it and put it out, leaving us with a smoke trail, which had no chance of being seen ashore in the darkness.

A tremendous report from a gun was then heard from close by, looking out we could just see the shape of a lightship, blurred in the blinding spray, then a couple of more cannon shots were heard, by this time we knew that someone somewhere was going to try and rescue us. But how? Well until you arrived we would have never known.

There are 120 souls aboard the Frederick, most of who were on the after deck; it was only us few that were asleep up forward that were on her bows. I pray to God that by some miracle they are saved.

We had just passed by the port side of the Brake Lightship, making good speed towards the shore, when, what all seamen dreaded, happened. A terrific bang came from under our bows, and a sudden inrush of water immediately followed; we had struck a piece of floating wreckage which had come from the Frederick. The sea was littered with huge timbers and planks, masts and sails, but in the dark and rough conditions we were unable to see anything floating on or just below the surface.

"She's struck something skipper!" I bellowed as I jumped to my feet to take a look at where the noise had come from. "There's water coming in her starboard side, quite fast as well skipper."

"Man the pump Tom, You mates get the buckets out and start bailing her out, I'm going to make for the light ship." bellowed the skipper as he turned the helm and came about into the teeth of the storm and sea.

Her head now beating up against the weather, and running on a port tack, we could clearly make out the damage that had occurred , every time she hit a sea it came rushing in through a hole in the port side, just below the water line, all the time we kept on a port tack she wasn't too bad, but sooner or later we would have to run on a starboard tack, if we wanted to get ashore, then the hole would be below the water level, making it hard to keep ahead of the inrush of water.

"What's the trouble Tom?" shouted the skipper taking another mouthful of water as a huge sea broke against our side.

"Looks like we've hit one of the Frederick's masts skipper, its torn a hole in her side wide enough to put a bucket in."

"Get the flares out Tom, set one off and warn the lightship we're in trouble, they'll be expecting us then." Shouted the skipper.

What a situation to get into, although it wasn't our fault. Launch to rescue a few souls, then have to require assistance ourselves; how embarrassing.

"She's going down fast skipper, we can't keep the water down, and its coming in faster than all of us can keep it out." I shouted over the roar of the wind.

."Keep it up mates, only a short distance to go before we haul up on the lightship. Do you're best." Replied the skipper.

No sooner had he said this than the shadow of a large boat under full sail came within sight on our port quarter. It was the Deal lifeboat, having launched earlier to render assistance to the Frederick. She must have been almost alongside us when we struck the submerged object, and seen our distress flare, turning straight away to come to our aid. A dim light could just be seen twinkering from the mizzen mast, disappearing every time the spray shot up in the air from the lifeboat's bows, as she beat rapidly towards us.

"What's the trouble skipper?" shouted the coxswain of the lifeboat as he pulled up astern of us.

"We've hit a bit of wreckage from the wreck, didn't see it in the dark, its cut a fair size hole in our bows mate. Were taking on a lot of water too, don't know how much longer we can keep her afloat. ."

The lifeboat quickly hove up alongside and passed a rope to us.

"Make her fast skipper." Shouted the lifeboat coxswain. "We'll take your passengers off, and then take you in tow for the shore."

Quickly the passengers we had rescued from the Frederick were transferred to the lifeboat which looking at, was already overloaded with survivors from the wreck.

The tow was secured and the lifeboat taking the strain turned her head for shore. As we came round to the strain of the tow a huge sea quartered us, filling the Lugger to the gunwales, tearing hard at the tow rope as the sudden weight increased. The lifeboat seeing what had happened immediately slackened their sheets, relieving the strain on the tow.

"Hang on lads, she's trying to go." Shouted the skipper. As another sea came inboard and sunk her completely beneath the gunwales. She had sunk but was lying submerged just below the sea level.

The lifeboat had now hauled up to us and offered to take us off and let the Lugger go, as it seemed she was now to become a total wreck.

"You take off my crew coxswain, Tom and myself will stay aboard and strap ourselves on safe. Just keep on towing us home, if she stays up and sort of afloat, then we have a chance to save her. Once you get her under way it will be easier then." the skipper said.

"Are you sure skipper?" came the reply.

"Aye that I am Cox. Get under way now."

With this final word the skipper cut the sheets and halyards off the Logger's mast, managed to knock out the pin that holds the mast and set it free. Away it went dragging the huge lug sail with it, being left far astern as the lifeboat slowly pulled us homeward. The Lugger now, had steadied on a more even keel, some of the water started rushing out over the stern. If we could hold her like this there might be a chance of saving her.

Frozen to the bone and soaking wet, we gathered all the oilskins and wet clothes up that we could find, these were wrapped around one of the wooden buckets that was still aboard, and with great difficulty, we managed to force the bucket into the hole in the Luggers side, wedging out the remainder of the gaps with the old cloth.

"That should hold it Tom." Said the skipper looking at me and shaking from head to toe with cold." We should be able to bail the water out of her now. Come on it will keep us warm pumping out, if nothing else."

Frantically we pumped and bailed out the Lugger relieving her of some of the load of water that was within her, gallon after gallon went over the side until she was but half full. We had approached the pier head and the lifeboat was now hailing us.

"Are you ok skipper? We've got to let you go now; can you manage to paddle her in from here?" the lifeboat coxswain said.

"I recon so." said the skipper. ."But we've lost our oars overboard, have you got a pair spare?"

The lifeboat hauled alongside and passed two of her long oars over to us, then bade us God's speed, and stood by while we rowed the half sunken boat towards the beach.

We swung the two long oars into the rowlocks and started to pull as hard as we could towards the shore, slowly the Lugger responded, gradually the Lugger's head swung round and the following seas picked her up and aiding us, pushed the Lugger towards the beach. The lifeboat now, seeing that we seemed to have the situation under control, bade us farewell, and proceeded at full speed to the shore, where her human cargo would be taken off and cared for.

Steadily we pulled on the oars, closer and closer we came, then we could make out the shapes of dozens of helpers waiting to haul us clear of the sea.

"Looks like plenty of helpers ashore skipper." I said in a stuttering voice, as the cold took away my breath.

"Aye that there is Tom, a good job as well, we'll need every bit of effort ashore to get her out of the water when she strikes.

There's a lot of weight in her now." The skipper said, as he prepared for beaching the Lugger.

The Lugger being so heavy in the water struck the shingle some yards out in the broken surf, stopping suddenly with a grinding crunch. The next sea caught her across the starboard beam and swung her round broadside, filling her again to the gunwales, she was now in danger of being broken up by the sea if she wasn't quickly pulled clear of the surf and drained of her heavy burden of water. The beach help quickly hooked her onto the winch wire and orders given to start hauling, almost at once the skipper jumped out and knocked out the bucket and clothes that we had used to plug the hole in her side, relieved of its position, a sudden rush of sea water came cascading out from within the Lugger, in a minute she was just about empty, a great relief, as now she could be hauled easily out of the sea and up the beach.

"Right Oh lads!" bellowed the skipper as loud as he could, while placing a wood under the Lugger's bows as she started to slowly move up the beach. ."Heave away lads, fast as you can now."

Every effort was put into getting the Lugger safely out of the crashing surf, eight hands were now manning the large capstan at the top of the beach, which steadily pulled her upwards, on and up she went, woods being placed beneath her bows as she moved upwards, foot by foot, over the high water bank she rose, her bows lifting high in the air, until all twenty tons of her wooden hull stood high and erect on her turntable, where she was finally made fast. A sorry state of a boat with masts gone and holed, it would be a week or so before this proud boat graced the coastline off Deal again.

All chocked up and secure the beach woods pulled up clear of the rising water, the hands all gathered at the Lugger's side, looking at the damage and listening to the story the skipper had to tell of our misadventure. Many onlookers had by now heard of our distress and like vultures on the kill, come to gloat at the misfortune we had encountered.

"Damned large hole you have there." Uttered a tall well dressed gentleman, who was viewing the situation from the promenade. ."You were lucky you didn't lose her in that sea." He uttered.

Many questions were asked and answered, the story of the rescue being given to all in its full account to the local times reporter, who, the skipper knew would pay handsomely for it if sales were good with his paper the next day.

By a coincidence the local boat builder of the town happened to be on the scene, and without losing any time spoke to the owner and secured the repair job. His estimate of repair was around three weeks time, that included a full inventory new mast and sail and new planking where the original had been damaged, not too long a time to wait before the Lugger would be in service again.

Meanwhile further to the North at the lifeboat station, the lifeboat had beached and been hauled up onto her turnstile, unloaded of her cargo of survivors and been re-launched again to the wreck of the Frederick. On the chance that some of the missing souls might still be onboard her, that's if she hadn't already gone to pieces. The boatmen's rooms were open and we, like the beach help made tracks for its welcoming doors, a warm fire would be found there, and a dry set of clothes, which would be most appreciated. Also by now in the boatmen's rooms would be all the survivors that had so far been rescued.

Entering the boatmen's rooms we saw dozens of people, women, children and men, all wrapped in thick blankets and drinking a cup of hot beverage. The local policeman was standing near the fireside talking to the very tall smartly dressed gentleman that had previously spoken to us on the beach. It later came to our attention that he was the owner of the ill fated ship, 'Frederick.' that had the misfortune of going aground and breaking up on the Brake sands.

Approaching the gentleman I saw that he too was somewhat drenched to the skin, thinking that he must have either been helping on the beach or a victim of the wreck I cautiously asked him of his name.

"Good day sir." I asked. ."Have you been involved in getting the Luggers ashore Sir, I noted you by our Lugger as we hauled up?"

The tall gentleman turned to me, and with a solemn look upon his face, looked me in the eyes, said

"I am the ill fated ship's owner lad, I have the unfortunate knowledge to be the last one saved from her, and I fear the rest of the poor souls onboard have perished. She had just about broken up by the time I left."

Other boatmen were meanwhile coming into the boatmen's rooms, dripping with water and frozen to the bone, one of the skippers came up to the skipper and myself, who had now left the tall gentleman to get some warmth from the fire.

"Lucky tonight wasn't you skipper? Didn't expect to see your Lugger ashore and hove up, the state she was in, must have had someone up there giving you a helping hand, eh!" He said

"Aye mate, she's got quite a bit of damage, but nothing that a few pieces of wood won't fix." He answered. ."Tell me mate, what's the position on the wreck, is she still in one piece? This tall gentleman here recons she's gone to pieces now?"

"Aye skipper, he's right." He replied." The gentleman came ashore in our Lugger, I'm afraid the ships gone, every bit of her broken to pieces."

"Did all the people managed to get saved mate." He asked solemnly. ."Not too many casualties I trust."

"Poor turnout skipper, all were saved except eight, they had been washed overboard when the Frederick struck the sand bank apparently, washed over the side. Not much hope for them I fear, the lifeboats out there now searching." He answered." One hundred and twelve were saved though; the Lord must be surely shining on us all, this wild night skipper. A miracle it is that more hadn't been drowned."

After a good warm up and change of clothes, our insides refreshed with a cup of hot broth, we left the boatmen's rooms. Making way to the beach, to view the damage, before going home for a few hours of well earned sleep.

"Good job we had a nice bit of cash from the earlier night's work lad." The skipper said to me, turning his head towards the sea and glancing out into the darkness. ."The money from that booty we bought in will come in handy now; we would be in a bad state without it, boat to repair and all that."

It was the skipper's misfortune of being skipper of the Lugger that night, and being in sole command, he took the responsibility for the damage incurred. This he had to pay for out of his own pocket. Quite a few pounds that would come to as well.

I answered the skipper somewhat sadly, he wasn't a bad sort of chap, although hard and tight with money at times, he always treated me right, I was always given a fair share of any thing he earn't, within reason. There must be some way in which I could help him with the costs of the repairs. I wonder?

I left the skipper and bade him good night, said I'd see him later in the morning. Making a turn round for the boatmen's rooms again, I took the task of finding the tall gentleman, the owner of the wrecked ship.

Within the boatmen's rooms I found the gentleman still sitting by the fire, talking to other members of some of the Deal boats crews.

"Pardon me for intruding Sir." I said to him." But may I have a word?"

I presented my questions to him, stating about the costs of repairing the Lugger that had rescued some of the ship's passengers, and how the skipper was expected to pay for the repairs from his own pocket."

The gentleman listened to my story with interest, letting me finish to the end. Then, in a gentle voice, he answered.

"Young man, I have taken care of the repairs with your boat builder, it's the most I could do after the service you all put in. Tell your skipper, it's all going to be paid for, and not to worry about a thing."

Astonished, and pleased I thanked the gentleman and bade him good day. Leaving for my house, and a couple of hours sleep.

The new day brought with it mixed fortunes for us, the Frederick, which had been wrecked during the night had gone to pieces on the incoming tide, nothing was left of her except. With the wind still blowing in from the east, wreckage had been washed ashore along the beach as far as one could see.

The skipper was standing by his boat shed when I arrived, puffing away on his pipe and glancing seaward.

"Good morning skipper, winds eased a bit." I said to him as I glanced along the beach at the masses of timber that had been washed ashore.

"Morning Tom, all refreshed now are you? There's plenty of pickings on the beach today, some good timber down there as well." He replied

"Skipper." I said to him." I was talking to that tall gentleman last night, after you left; he's told me that he is going to have the Lugger repaired, so you won't have to pay for it out of your pocket after all. In gratitude for the services we put in, rescuing those poor fellows off his ship."

"Aye I know Tom he's been up here this morning, I've already spoken to him, thanks all the same." he replied. ."There's a ten pound note for everyone involved in last nights rescue work as well. Should come in nice and handy Tom."

This money would more than make up for any loss we had incurred from not being able to go to sea in the Lugger on services for the next few weeks. Although the skipper's own boat was still in service for fishing. That's if the weather ever came nice again. Besides an easterly wind on these shores was no good to anyone, the fish disappeared and it was almost impossible to try and go drift netting for herring, the gear and boat would be blown ashore.

The following six weeks saw the wind constantly blowing fresh from the East, nothing had put to sea for some time now and the herring season was coming to an end. Hopefully this spell of unusual weather would change before the sprat season started; otherwise things were going to become very hard.

The Lugger had been repaired, and once again sat proudly upon her stocks, waiting for the call of a distress flare, or perhaps to take a pilot out to a stray ship that might decide to venture through the inner part of the sands. Who knows what the next day would bring.

******

Chapter Six

A Good Day's Work

The winter had been one of the worst in my memory, giving little or no break in its bitter cold easterly winds; winds from which this part of the coast presented more than one problem.

From late December until mid March bitter cold winds and heavy snow battered the houses of Deal, covering all but the masts of the boats along the foreshore, boats which had been pulled clear up to the houses as far as possible, thus avoiding the wrath of the seas as they pounded endlessly against the shingle beach, grabbing and clawing large amounts of stones from all along the foreshore with never ending might, leaving many of the plots where the boats were usually stationed, bare of stones and in many places with a drop off the sea wall where the shingle had been completely scoured out.

Apart from a couple of heads of sail being driven onto the treacherous Goodwin Sands, nothing else had happened along the foreshore, even these two large ships which had the misfortune of becoming stranded on the sands didn't give many boatmen a chance to earn a crust, after all, what boat could launch into the teeth of an easterly gale and survive? Not our small craft that's for sure. The large Luggers however were able to launch, and aiding the rescue of the unfortunate crews and the salvage of some valuable cargo did alright for themselves.

The Downs anchorage off Deal had been almost deserted throughout the winter; shipping having passed to the east'ard of the Goodwin Sands, not stopping or anchoring in the Downs, which in an easterly blow was too exposed, threatening to blow ashore any ship that was foolish enough to try her luck.

March was closing to its end and with the moon waning the wind had decided to abate. The plot or position of the beach where the boat which I formed part of the crew was opposite North Street, close to the Seagirt House, further north along the beach from where I worked with the skipper, his boat was at the top of Brewer street. It was common practice for a crew and skipper to take charge of another boat in a season if the work wasn't there for their own boat. And this time the skipper and I had joined another boat, as this had work and we didn't, ours was far too small to be launched in bad weather, and besides our boat was limited to the distance it could travel. We also, were now having to take another crew member on board to help sail her, now we had to call the skipper by his name, 'Harry', not to the liking of the skipper, but the other crew member, Dick was his name, was also a skipper. This would hopefully stop any confusion if skipper was used to address one of them.

Much of the beach had been eroded leaving a lot of work barrowing loads of beach from the low water to the high water mark, a job we all hated, but the boat had to be set once more on its turntable with a good beach behind it ready to launch. It was impossible to launch any boat over the steep shingle banks that had been caused by the scouring motion of the easterly winds. Now a large bank of shingle was building up some eighty feet below the highest high water mark, so this had to be removed.

It was the last day of March, early morning when activity once again started to bustle along the beach. The skipper, or should I say Harry, and the other crew member of the boat, Dick, and I, had arrived on the scene and were discussing the possibility of getting the boat back on her berth. A long glance at the situation and careful quiet thoughts ran through all our heads.

"Well mates! It's no good us standing around here like three little old women is it? We've got lots to do before we can go afloat; for a start lets get the barrows and drag some of the beach back up here, once we get the boat back on her stocks we can see then what's in store for us, the winds finished now for a while I recon, about time as well, another couple of weeks of this and we would all be starving. What'll you say mates?" Harry said as he turned his weather beaten face towards us.

"I should imagine you're about right Harry." that was the skippers name just to remind you in case we forget. ."There are not many times you're wrong Harry are there? That's about right isn't it Dick?" I replied as I turned to my crew mate and winked.

"Yes Tom, he's always right, anyway the beach has got to be brought up here somehow otherwise it is going to be impossible to get the old girl afloat."

By the old girl he meant the boat, this was just a way of calling the boat a nice sort of name, her real name was The Mary-Anne. Not one of the Lugger class type but a good enough sea boat once she was afloat, having a length of thirty six feet and rigged fore and aft with mizzen, main and jib she wanted some catching too in a breeze.

"You get the beach sorted out mates and I'll sort out the old girl ready for work." Harry said." I should reckon we'll get afloat easy tomorrow."

"Right oh!" myself and Dick answered, mumbling beneath our breath, as Harry put us to work on the heavy tasks, while he took the easy job of preparing the boat. Nothing had changed there.

The long tedious task of barrowing beach up and down began, load after load, and ton after ton. By mid morning we had finished, the beach was leveled off nicely and looked a picture, a gradual sloping ramp had been made, it would be easy to launch now. We were now both a bit worse for wear, and putting our barrows away we approached Harry to see what he had in mind for us for the rest of the day. One things for sure, he wouldn't let us have a rest yet.

Dick and I leant over the Mary-Anne's rails totally exhausted, and panting from lack of breath, gained Harry's attention.

."Finished Harry!" We both said together as the sweat ran down our faces into our mouths. ."What now?"

"Come on then Tom, you get the woods laid while Dick helps me get the nets back aboard her."

The nets had been stowed in two large beach boxes to stop them from being carried away during the previous gales that had been lashing the beach, the lids of which were quickly opened with Harry and Dick rapidly stowing them in the Mary-Anne's hold, whilst I greased and laid the woods ready to release the boat from her resting place, returning her to the beach where she normally sat proud and ready, a picture of beauty at the least glance. I was just laying the last wood in its position when Harry shouted out at me.

"How are you getting on Tom? Put plenty of grease on the woods mate, otherwise we will never be able to move her."

."Just finished Harry, all greased up well and sorted, ready when you are."

"Right Dick get the slip chain on her and hitch her up to the winch lad, don't want her going afloat without us do we?"

Dick rove the chain through the reeving hole and made ready the winch whilst I took the chocks from under her bilges. She came down on her bilge keel with a heavy crash as the chock was released, moving seaward at the same time.

."Hold her Dick, steady now." shouted Harry." She's alive and running."

Before he had hardly stopped speaking, the winch wire suddenly tightened with the force of the Mary-Anne's weight straining heavily on it, causing it to quiver in the light afternoon air. The Mary-Anne came suddenly to a halt as the winch stopped her from rushing further seaward.

"Ok Dick, ease her down. Watch them woods Tom, steady now; steady."

The Mary-Anne slowly slid over the greased woods towards the sea, running with ease down the smooth gradient we had made of the beach.

"Hold her there Dick." The winch brake went on and the Mary-Anne's progress was arrested.

"Come on Tom get those woods down." Said Harry, as he bent down to move one of the large setting woods.

I picked up the other end of the setting wood and between us we managed to place it in front of the Mary-Anne's bows, then the second wood was moved and placed twenty feet further up the beach. These two large woods were what the Mary-Anne would sit on after she had been turned around, and where she would proudly wait until she was ready to be released into the sea.

"Right Tom lets go and help Dick wind her up, come on mate."

The three of us put our weight onto the winch handle and started turning it. Slowly the Mary-Anne inched her way up the beach and on to the setting boards, leaning over proudly on her port beam.

"Hold her there!" shouted Harry.

The pool was thrown over and with a clang the winch took her weight, the Mary-Anne slipped back a couple of inches then stopped.

"Come on mates get her up on an even keel, all together now heave!"

Grunting and moaning we put our backs under the port rail of the Mary-Anne and with all our might together heaved her upright.

"Chock her up Tom, quickly now, we can't hold her up forever." Harry said, puffing like an old man.

I kicked the chock into position and with relief we let her go. She wasn't a light weight boat for her size some twenty tons of solid elm and oak, and very strong and heavily built. She sat on her chocks with her bows proudly facing the sea, ready for the command of." Let go." when it came, eagerly waiting to go about her duty. Harry called us both over to him; he was bent double and gasping for his breath.

"You know I think I'm getting too old for this here lark." He said still struggling for his breath." I'm sixty now you know."

We just laughed and commented on his age, not understanding how getting old can take the stuffing out of you, after all we were both but teenagers.

"That's better." said Harry as he slowly straightened up his body, breathing somewhat easier. ."That's better, right now here's what we are going to do."

He went on to explain how we would go afloat on the slack in the morning, about four a.m. make our way out to the west Goodwin banks, shoot the trammel nets then go trawling on the brake sands until late afternoon. We would then haul the dog trammels, resetting them if the fishing was good.

"Are you both alright with that mates?" he asked." Hopefully if the weather stays like this it should be a fine day."

"Yes Harry." I replied quietly as Dick stood beside me nodding his head in agreement.

"Right then; I'll see you both in the morning don't be late now."

With this we said our farewells and made tracks to our own homes, awaiting the time when we would hopefully go afloat and the prospects of some fish and money again.

Three in the morning soon came around. A quick cup of warm tea, clothes on, and I was away to the beach. It was a cold frosty night with puddles of water frozen in the Gullies in the middle of the road, shining like mirrors in the moonlight. Arriving at the Mary-Anne I found Harry and Dick already waiting both slouched across the winch in deep conversation.

"Good morning all!" I exclaimed as I drew near them, and rested my shoulder against the bows of the Mary-Anne.

"Ah! Hello Tom, have a good night eh? Thought you weren't coming, overlay did you?" Harry sarcastically commented to me.

I didn't take much notice of Harry's remarks, he was always a bit sarcastic if I turned up late, but no harm was meant.

"Well Harry I thought if I turned up early like I have this morning and you are here before me, well surely you've got the boat and woods ready. After all it's only half past three, all ready to launch is she, saved me a job have you?" I replied rudely.

Harry and Dick went quiet for a minute then Dick, in his usual quiet manner spoke to me.

"Not to worry Tom we saw you coming up the beach, we were behind you and shot up the side street a bit smartish, thought we'd have one up on you." Dick said.

"Yes well I didn't take much notice of what you both said anyway. I've got used to Harry and his remarks now, after sailing with him for the past five years. You'll learn that Dick."

I walked past the two of them and started to lay the woods down the beach not saying another word. The beach rustled behind me, Harry had gone to the boat and climbed aboard and Dick was standing by the slip chain. I laid the woods as far as the high water bank and no further as the tide was rising., and hadn't much further to go before it was high water. Making my way back to the Mary-Anne I saw that Harry had raised the mizzen and jib sails in readiness to launch.

"All ready Harry, the tides coming up so I laid the woods to the top of the bank, they won't wash away when we're afloat, and hopefully some one will pull them up in the morning for us?"

"Good Tom get aboard and stand by with the main halyard. Are you ready to let go Dick?"

"Ready when you are Harry."

"Let go."

Harry's voice boomed out across the beach like a cannon going off, most probably waking half the town.

Away she went the chain clanging as it rushed through the ruffle hole, releasing the Mary-Anne from her mooring. With a clamber Dick appeared above the stern, he had to jump aboard after letting go or stay ashore. This was achieved quite easily, as on the stem and stern of the Mary-Anne; blocks of wood were bolted, making a sort of step up to the top of the gunwales. On letting go the slip chain all Dick had to do was jump on the bottom step and climb up onto the aft deck. He was then safely aboard.

Quickly the Mary-Anne gathered speed rushing over the greasy boards, she left the beach and for some yards flying through the air as she rushed over the high water bank, crashing back into the beach some yards further down. Grating and grinding her way through the soft shingle as she made her way to the sea.

"Hang on tight Dick." Harry shouted.

Dick was still hanging over the stern, unable to gain entry aboard as the Mary-Anne had taken to launching herself at a greater speed than usual.

With an almighty splash she forced her way through the breakers and sat upright on the swell as it ran beneath the keel. Gently she heeled over to starboard as the light easterly wind took charge of the sails. A shouting and mumbling was coming from the stern as Dick struggled to clamber aboard. I quickly rushed aft and gave him a hand

"Alright now Dick? Come on mate I'll give you a hand." I said as I pulled at Dick's shoulders and helped him inboard.

"Only just, blooming fingers have gone numb with cold, thought I were going to fall off as she ran over the bank, damn close." replied Dick.

With Dick safely aboard, we hoisted the mainsail, gracefully the old boat heeled over as the wind filled the vast expanse of canvas that was hanging from her masts, slowly and steadily she gathered way, steadily increasing her speed as the breeze caressed every bit of the tanned sails. Within a few minutes we had cleared the pier head, and were heading off to the fishing grounds we had decided to fish.

"Come on you two, we're going about now, get on those sheets lads." Harry commanded as he stood firmly in the stern steering the Mary-Anne.

No sooner had Harry shouted his orders, than he pushed the tiller over, down came the mainsail and up it went again on the port side of the mast. Over she laid again, heeling to the gusts which came across the gentle breeze.

"Right you two, the tides on the ebb and the winds in the east, so we shouldn't have to tack again until we reach the west Goodwin banks. You can have a rest if you desire."

With relief Dick and I settled down amidships, while Harry skippered us out to the grounds where the nets would be shot. The time passed very quickly as there wasn't much of a distance to travel, and then before we knew it we saw the Brake lightship fall astern of us and the boom of Harry's voice breaking the silence of the night.

"Come on you two we're here, look lively now; let's get this gear shot and fishing."

Dick and I jumped to our feet just as the mainsail fell to the deck; Harry had released the halyard without any warning, not saying he was in a hurry.

."Lower that jib Dick. Throw over the first dhan Tom, look sharp there."

As the jib fell the head of the Mary-Anne was swung round to the sou'east, over went the first dhan followed sharply by the first anchor. With a rattling and clanging the nets were pulled overboard by the rushing of the tide. One end now anchored to the seabed, over went the second anchor followed by the wash line and dhan, that was the first fleet over and fishing. We drifted for some fifty yards then the first dhan of the second fleet was thrown overboard followed by the anchor. Out rushed the nets over the port rail, rapidly coming up on the anchor which was thrown overboard, again followed by a dhan, this operation was repeated until all the nets were safely shot.

"Not much water here Harry, it can't be more than eight feet deep." I said looking at the turbulence the shallow water was causing around us.

"That's alright Tom, nothing to hurt here." Harry answered reassuringly.

Ten fleets of nets were set on the west Goodwin banks, each fleet having four nets to it. These nets were anchored to the bottom and were used for catching Huss only, or spotted dog fish as some land lubbers call them.

Harry remarked how good the fishing should be after all the easterly wind. Huss's were always abundant in easterlies and the water being thick would certainly aid our catching.

"Hoist the jib Dick; get ready with the main Tom." Harry shouted, as he took his position at the tiller once again.

Harry's orders were instantly obeyed, up went the jib and the tiller was put hard over to port and around came her head to the nor'ard.

"Hoist the main mates, make it sharp now, we want to get the trawl down as soon as we can."

As the main sail was raised the Mary-Anne once again made headway gathering speed with every roll. Harry ran alongside the fleets of trammel nets taking bearings from the shore as we passed them. This area was notorious in easterly winds for having fog, so time and distance bearings were also taken, that way if anything happened we would be able to find them again easily. We made sail for the Brake lightship, timing the minutes from the nets to the lightship, this would give us our distance out should the fog come in.

"Right." shouted Harry. "Got them."

By this he meant he had enough information stashed away in that brain of his to find the nets again no matter what the weather. We hailed the Brake lightship as we ran alongside her, attracting the attention of one of the crew members who was fishing with a hand line over her stern.

"Morning aboard, how's the fishing tonight?" I shouted to one of the crew men on board her as we came up under the Lightship's stern.

A face glanced over the lightship's side, almost covered completely with a balaclava hat. He was pulling in a hand line which seemed to have a nice fish on the end of it.

"Who's away there?" shouted the man as he peeped through the hole in his helmet. ."Oh it's the Mary-Anne is it? You're about early Harry. What's up the wife kicked you out old feller?"

Harry just laughed at the comment made by the chap on the lightship, was his cousin Bill so a joke between them went deservingly unnoticed.

"No I left on my own free will this time Bill, how's the fishing going?"

The men on the lightship spent a lot of time fishing; there wasn't much else to do anyway, stuck two miles off shore on a ship with no means of propulsion, just rolling around, most likely getting the odd wave from a passing passenger vessel.

"Not bad Harry, there's few Huss and cod about; we've got a couple of good size plaice as well." The reply came.

"Good on you Bill, we're going to have a tow up and down the banks around you for a few hours, see if we can pick up a bit of flat fish while the trammels are fishing, don't go much on our chances, but it's worth a try. See you later."

With a wave we hove in tight on the sheets and gathered way again, soon reaching the broken water of the Brake sands some four hundred yards north of the lightship.

The trawl was a twelve foot beam trawl and a good catcher as well, without losing way we lowered the trawl over the starboard side and down into the sea, rapidly the tow rope was paid out, coming up tight with a shudder as it reached its end, and the full weight of the trawl on the seabed was taken. The Mary-Anne took the strain and with every bit of sail set slowly started to pull the trawl along the seabed.

An hour passed by quickly and before we knew it we were up alongside the North West Goodwin buoy about a two and a half mile distance from where we had first put the trawl over the side. The ebb tide had now eased, with the first trickle of flood beginning to run through, the seas too had become much larger as the tide had risen, some of which were towering in towards the shore like giant cliffs again, a sure sign that the easterly wind wasn't yet ready to leave us.

"Looks like we've plenty more wind to come yet." Harry shouted from the stern, as he leant over the aft thwart and began to slacken off the main sheet.

"Let's get her up mates. Right oh Tom, start hauling."

As the commands came across from the stern Harry slackened off the main sheets, allowing the Mary-Anne to hold abeam of the wind. Dick and I started hauling in the thick manila warp which was connected to the trawl, the rope came in rapidly at first, but as we took the full strain of the trawl we came to a sudden stop.

"We can't move her Harry, something heavy in her by the feels of it."

"Alright Tom let me get a hold there." Said Harry as he took a position between us and started to pull on the rope.

."Haul in as she rolls down mates, that's it. Hold her now, right as she rolls down haul in."

We let the sea do the work of hauling for us, stopping the trawl running back overboard as the Mary-Anne rolled up, and then hauling in as she ran her gunwales under.

"Here she comes Harry; one more heave will do it." I said looking over at the side to see where the trawl was.

"Tie the beams off Tom, quick about it now, don't want to let her go back to the bottom."

I tied the aft end of the beam off while Dick tied the fore end of the beam off, thus stopping the trawl from returning back to the seabed. The cod end was hanging tightly down below our keel; we had picked up something very heavy indeed.

"Right Tom get the tackle hooked on to the back strop, that's it; hook her in now; good!"

We had managed to hook the block and tackle into the back strop which lifted the cod end aboard, the lines were tightened up and the full weight of the net came down onto the lifting tackle.

"All together now." Shouted Harry," After six Heave! Ready, one two six Heave!"

Slowly the net raised itself above the water and started to come over the rail. The Mary-Anne took on a good list with the weight that was hanging over her side.

"Once more mates and we've got her, altogether, one two six heave!"

The cod end cleared the rail and rolled inboard, righting our list instantly. I let the tackle go thus letting the net fall onto the deck. What a sight!

"Come on Tom get the cod end open, lets get her emptied and see how we've done."

Quickly I released the knot that held the cod end closed, and with a jelly like rush hundreds of fish splattered over the deck, covering our legs to some six inches deep.

"Will you look at that Harry." I exclaimed excitedly. ."What a catch, didn't expect to see that amount of fish?"

"Sure is a good one Tom. Come on now you two lets get the net cleared and back overboard again, hurry up."

I retied the cod end and threw it over the side; Dick unlashed the beam while Harry tightened in the sheets and once more got the Mary-Anne underway.

"Let her go Dick." Came the voice from the stern as Harry headed the Mary-Anne's bows back to the south'ard, reversing the tow we had just taken, while Dick payed out the tow rope until it came up tight.

"All away Harry." cried Dick. ."She's up taught and fishing again."

With the trawl over the side and fishing again, Dick and I then started to gut the catch, then wash and box it. It was a good haul, taking us nearly an hour to clear the fish, which consisted mainly of large plaice with a few Dover soles and small codling.

"What have we got Tom?" asked Harry.

"At a guess I'd say about a hundred and ten stone Harry, good days work eh?" I replied.

"Aye if we get a couple more hauls like that one we won't complain." Said Dick as he lifted up his head and gave out a big grin.

Just as we had finished clearing away Harry had decided to haul again. We had come up close to the Brake lightship already, and the flood tide was now running strong, with a freshened wind. For some reason the easterly's always freshened up at high water, why I don't know.

"Right mates lets have a look." Harry shouted with an eager expression on his face.

The main sheet was released and we started hauling, the warp came in easily at first as the Mary-Anne drifted back over it on the strong tide, then suddenly up tight it came, as we took the strain of the trawl on the other end. With a couple of flicks I took a turn around the Samson post, securing the trawl from pulling the rope back seaward as we slowly drifted down on the tide. The three of us struggled again to get the trawl inboard; steadily upward it came foot by foot, until after some minutes of heavy heaving and pulling, exhausted, we pulled it to the Mary-Anne's rail.

"Make her fast mates, get the tackle." came the orders, as if we didn't know what to do.

Once more we had a heavy load, not so much as the first haul but a good haul just the same, over the rail came the cod end, which was quickly emptied onto the deck.

"Must have a good fifty stone here Harry." I remarked." Not so good as the first haul, but still a good catch."

"Aye Tom, not so much, but still a good haul. Come on lets get her over again."

Once more the trawl was shot, the fish cleared and another haul made. We had six tows in all, catching some three hundred stone of good large plaice and about forty stone of mixed fish. A good weeks fishing in a day. The last haul came aboard and was quickly cleared away, Harry then decided to go back to the trammel nets and haul them before dark set in upon us.

By now the tide had fallen and the ebb was running again to the south'ard. We hove up on the first dhan picked it up and started hauling. Harry kept the Mary-Anne slowly heading up to the nor'ard, taking off some of the strain.

Up came the first head of the first net, with Huss's hanging like grapes from the meshes. Yard after yard of net came aboard, with Dick and myself taking turns in hauling, the nets were full of Huss, hardly a mesh was empty, the first fleet aboard and the anchor and dhan in we made headway for the second fleet.

"Grab holds of that dhan Dick, right make her fast." Harry said as he turned the Mary-Anne's head towards the dhan.

As Dick made the Mary-Anne fast to the anchor of the second fleet Harry and myself dropped all the sails. We were going to lie too for a while and clear all the fish from the nets, then re-shoot them again. It took but a quarter of an hour for the three of us to clear the fish from the first fleet. Twelve score of Huss; a good haul.

"Let's get them back over the side mates, up sail and let go the anchor!" shouted Harry eagerly.

The Mary-Anne made headway to the nor'ard once more. The nets were re-shot and the second fleet hauled. This proved just as good as the first fleet. Again it was cleared of fish and re-shot.

The whole procedure was repeated with every fleet until we reached the end, all the nets being re-shot, these would be hauled again on the first tide in the morning. We had on board over a hundred score of Huss, along with a dozen good size turbot.

Dark had fallen upon us now as we made our way shore ward, a fair wind and following sea bringing us quickly to our berth on Deal beach. The shore was alive with boatmen all rushing around getting the wire and woods ready for our landing, a good sight as it meant we had less work to do, and we could haul up and get cleared away quicker.

"Quite a crowd ashore Harry," I said staring through the dark at the shadows scuffling about on the shore.

"Aye Tom sure is, they all want a feed of the fish I expect, look how low we're lying in the water. Gives us away don't it."

As Harry said this the Mary-Anne's bows struck the beach, heaving her out of the sea by at least a third of her length, and rolling over gently onto her starboard bilge. We had beached.

One of the old boatmen stood shakily at the bows with the winch hook in his hands, Dick lowered the reeving chain down from the Mary-Anne's bows into his grasp; and with not too much hurry he hooked it onto the winch hook. Waving his arm Dick signaled to the beach help to start winding on the winch. The message was carried to the winch, and the great wire began taking the strain of the Mary-Anne, slowly pulling her clear of the water and upwards to her berth. It was almost completely dark now and only the faint outline of the men on the winch could be seen.

With a groaning and creaking the winch took the Mary-Anne's weight, pulling her bows up onto the greased wood that had been thrust beneath it, making the weight of the boat and the catch easier to pull up the beach. Six burly men had manned the winch, three on each handle, but even with six men this was no easy task, twenty tons of boat and the weight of the fish. But slowly she inched her way towards the seafront and her mooring blocks. The greasy woods were being regularly placed beneath her bows as she moved herself landwards.

Old Harry had jumped out of the Mary-Anne and was standing on the beach chatting to the old boatman and was giving him a bit of flannel.

"You tell them." I heard him say.

He had obviously told the old boy a pack of lies as to where we'd found the fish, not remembering that we were spied on from the shore by the other boat's crews, after all, we were only around two miles out.

The Mary-Anne came to a sudden stop on her chocks, she was up and secured, crowds gathered around to witness the amazing catch we had, mouths opening in astonishment.

"Done well old Harry haven't you?" one of the boatmen commented.

"Yes we caught a bit today; it'll keep us from going hungry for a day or two anyway." Harry replied.

The catch was unloaded and put on the hand carts ready for the buyers to come, although most of the fish were laid in boxes on the beach, as the carts were quite full. Questions were asked to all of us, everyone trying to find out exactly where we had been, without much success though, old Harry just kept saying.

"Oh out there, you saw us, you saw where we were."

Much haggling and bargaining took place during the next hour, with the best prices being secured for the catch. There hadn't been a bit of good fish landed for weeks, so it was in high demand.

"Right mates." Harry said, as he came across to Dick and I "Right mates here's the score."

He went on to tell us what we were going to do in the morning.

"We launch at four to go and haul trammels in but we're not taking the trawl, they'll all be afloat out there tonight, we won't get a good tow, ok see you both at four then."

With this he left us to finish clearing up and getting the Mary-Anne ready for her launch in the morning, then as usual he made his way to his local pub where he would spend the next couple of hours before going home.

It didn't take Dick and I long to get the jobs we had to do, done, Dick and I bid each other good night and went our ways, a few hours sleep would go down just nice.

The night went by quickly with four o'clock coming round far too soon. As planned we all arrived up the beach, and set about turning the Mary-Anne round ready for launch.

The remainder of the snow that was lying on the ground had rapidly melted in the last twenty four hours and dry patches could be seen taking over from the muddy puddles. The wind was still fresh from the east and bitter cold to the touch but the sea wasn't too rough. I glanced along the foreshore towards the pier, noticing that a number of the larger boats had left their berths.

"See that Harry! Quite a few of the other boats have gone away tonight."

Harry just turned to me and grinned, as if by some uncanny way he knew what to expect.

"Well Tom, why do you reckon I said we won't take the trawl with us today? I said yesterday we wouldn't get a berth did I not?"

"Aye that you did Harry, but they're nearly all afloat aren't they?"

."Never mind Tom, we've got our trammels to empty, they'll be full enough this morning. How are you getting on Dick, nearly ready?"

"When you are." Answered Dick as he finished lashing the slip chain through the Mary-Anne's ruffle hole.

"Right let's get afloat." Ordered Harry as he gave a last inspection down the beach to make sure all was in order.

Harry then placed the ladder against the side of the boat, climbed up to the gunwales and clumsily clambered in, immediately making his way aft to hoist the mizzen sail, Dick had taken up position on the slip chain and I climbed aboard and positioned myself amidships ready to hoist the mainsail.

"Let go." the order came.

The chain rattled and banged as it rushed through the ruffle hole, releasing the Mary-Anne from its grip, Dick scrambled over the quarter and joined me amidships as the Mary-Anne started her journey to the sea.

It was calmer this morning, so no woods were laid below the high water bank, these were not needed anyway on calm days as normally the speed of the boat would take her to the water's edge without any problems The Mary-Anne rushed seaward without a minute to spare, thrusting herself into the cold sea with such momentum that she went some hundred yards seaward before we were able to gain a foothold and hoist the sail. The main and jib were set and Harry set his course towards the west Goodwin, his weather beaten face staring into the twilight of the morning, eager to find out where all the other boats had gone.

It was a good hour before we hove up on the Brake lightship, the tide was running strong on the ebb and with the light breeze we needed every inch of canvas for the Mary-Anne to make headway against it.

On approaching the Brake lightship we could see a figure standing on the deck, dressed in yellow oilskins and a yellow sou'wester on his head. It was Harry's cousin, was looking over the side of the lightship; just as if he was expecting us to arrive at that particular moment.

"Good morning Harry." Shouted Bill from the lightship." You won't get a berth out there this morning; it looks like all the fleet from Deal is working the grounds where you were fishing yesterday."

He gave a sort of cunning snigger as if he knew what Harry was going to say.

"You needn't worry Bill, we're not working there this morning, and we've still got the old dog nets set on the west Goodwin. Catch you later."

As he shouted these last words we quietly and steadily sailed past the lightship, Harry wasn't stopping to talk to his cousin this morning, we had nets to haul and reset before the flood tide started running. Another half an hours sailing saw us hauling up on the first dhan bringing it onboard and commencing hauling the nets, leaving Harry to steer the Mary-Anne. Over the rail they came by the dozen, Huss after Huss, scores of them.

"We've done alright again this morning by the looks of it Harry." I shouted.

He never answered, we hauled and shot the first fleet, then the second and carried on until all the nets had been hauled, cleared and all reset again.

"What have we got Tom? Came a voice from the stern as we finished filling the last ox with Huss.

We'd been counting as we hauled so knew exactly how many fish we had in each box therefore counting the boxes it was easy to work out how many fish we had on board.

"How many did you get Dick?" I whispered quietly so that Harry couldn't hear me.

Fifty one and a half score." He said in a quiet voice back to me as if he knew I was going to try and wind Harry up by giving him the wrong tally. With my count added to this I answered Harry's question.

"One hundred and eleven score and six in total Harry." I shouted

"Is that so mates, well if you add another twenty score to that it might be right, might it not?"

We had tried to deceive old Harry, but the old devil had been counting as well.

"Ah you're right Harry one hundred and thirty one score and six, plus twenty three large turbot, four boxes of cod and three parts a box of plaice. Not bad eh!"

"A very good day's work lads, we can't complain at that, come on lets get ashore."

With this all sail was set and under the light easterly breeze we slowly made our course towards the shore set. We beached without any mishap or problems, hauled up and cleared away the fish to the buyers.

."Well mates should do well again in the morning; all the time the wind stays like this we'll have a good catch."

"Good." Piped up Dick."Good, its about time we earn't some money, the previous skipper of the Mary-Anne wasn't much good at all, spent most of his time drinking in the ale house. I'm glad you took over as skipper Harry."

I think he was getting a bit fed up with fishing owing to the fact we hadn't had a pay week since Christmas.

"You won't know what to spend your money on next week Dick, will you?" Harry said to him jokingly. ."Come on let's go and see what the other boats have got."

The first of the smaller boats was just coming ashore after a night on the grounds where we caught the fish the previous day. We wandered along and sat on a beach box chatting to a couple of other old boatmen while one of the boats was being hauled up the beach.

"She's up and fast Harry." Dick piped up."Shall we have a look and see what they've got?"

With this we all stood up and walked over to the boat, leant over the rail, looked aboard and said nothing. Harry was staring at the skipper, grinning slightly below the pipe which he had just lit up.

."Not so good Freddie didn't find em eh?" he said struggling to contain his expressions.

Freddie turned to him angrily and replied.

"It would have been alright if some other person hadn't been so greedy and caught the lot."

Freddie only had one box of mixed fish, and on seeing all the other boats land the results were very much the same. No fish.

."Well mates, it looks like we hit them before they moved off, doesn't it?"

"Aye Harry." We both answered, with large grins beaming over our faces.

Harry knew like us that after our grand catch of plaice, that any fish still left would be gone the next day. The fish had been lying in the deep trenches between the sand banks sheltering from the pounding seas, which now were much calmer, the fish had moved off. Where to, was anyone's guess?

The next two months saw some good catches of Huss coming ashore from the Mary-Anne, with the occasional break when the winds turned out of the east and into the west'ard, which was no good for trammel fishing.

****

Chapter seven

__Behind the Goodwins__

The cold winter and spring passed by with amazing speed, aided by the fact I suppose that we had during the last few weeks, very little time to call our own, apart from the odd day or two when the winds veered to the west'ard bringing a stop to dogging. These winds never produced any good catches at all whilst trammeling for Huss; why I never knew, but the Huss just seemed to disappear.

With the coming of June, the winds had now become more frequent to the westerly quarter, a change of fishing methods had to be sought.

There had, in the last few days been a few French drifters, lying in Ramsgate harbour, and by all accounts these had found good mackerel fishing at the back of the Goodwin Sands. No-one had however seen anything of their catches, although their boats had been reported to be lying rather low in the water, suggesting that they did contain a heavy catch of something.

It was on a warm June Monday morning that, while Harry, Dick and myself were standing by the old Mary-Anne looking eastward out onto a flat calm summer looking sea, that Harry decided to change the fishing gear that was being used in the Mary-Anne. This meant that we were going to try a different method of fishing.

"Now my lads, this here is what we are going to do." Said Harry as he went on explaining to us what we were going to go out and try and catch.

It appeared that we were going to have a go at mackerel fishing, as Harry seemed to think there was something in the Frenchmen's holds that they were keeping secret.

The dog trammels were washed up and hung out on poles to dry in the sun, dhans and anchors were coiled and put into the storehouse, and the Mary-Anne was given a lick of linseed oil, thus keeping her bright and ready for a season afloat again.

Mackerel nets were broken out of the storehouse, where for the last ten months they had been lying. To put it in plain English the nets were taken from the store house ready for use.

Thirty nets were used in the fleet, all joined together to make nearly one mile and a half of net when shot. These were again drift nets with buoys secured to the headline every four fathoms, thus keeping them up on the surface, hanging like a giant curtain when shot and catching everything that swam into them, very similar to the herring drift nets used except they were deeper and had a slightly larger mesh size.

It took almost four days to prepare the nets and boat for the start of the mackerel fishing, during which time visual evidence of mackerel had been seen; one of the charter boats with a party of anglers had been fortunate enough to find a few.

"Saturday!" shouted Harry suddenly. All went quiet. "Saturday." He shouted again without warning.

."Saturday what?" Dick replied with amazement as we were at a loss as to what Harry was talking about.

"Saturday's the day; we're going off Saturday to try and catch some mackerel lads ok?"

We both nodded knowing now what he meant by Saturday. "What time Harry?" I asked.

."The tides at ten; we'll launch at seven and catch the tide across the Gull's to the north sands head, we'll give it a try at the back of the sands, that's where the Frenchmen seem to be working."

It was Friday today so it didn't give us much time to get ourselves sorted out, ready for the long trip to the back of the sands, this would be a two or three day trip, as it was quite a long way offshore.

"Fancy starting on a Saturday." I mumbled to Dick."The end of the week, he must be crazy, a normal skipper would go away Sunday for the Monday market."

"What's that Tom? If you don't like the work we can go without you." Answered Harry, as he turned his face angrily towards me. He had heard the comment I had made to Dick and didn't seem too pleased.

"No, I was just kidding Harry, I'll be there don't worry."

Harry knew as well as I did that my berth would be quickly filled should I disapprove of his command. His was always the top earning boat from fishing and many would jump at the chance to ship on with him.

The Mary-Anne ready Harry leaned against her bow, filled his pipe and lit it, blowing clouds of thick smoke over Dick and me.

"You can go now." He said blowing out another cloud of smoke in our direction." See you at seven sharp!"

With this Dick and I jumped out of the Mary-Anne and bid Harry farewell till the morning tide.

"I'll see you later," said Dick as he strolled off towards his local ale house.

Dick loved a beer and sadly this is where most of his money went. I however, although indulging in the odd one, kept well clear. It was my ambition to own my own boat one day, so carefully I saved every penny I could. Saturday morning came and we set sail as planned.

It was a calm sunny morning with hardly a ripple on the surface, bad news for us crewmen. Launching went off without a hitch, sails were set and the worst bit came, no wind meant rowing.

"Get those oars over the side." shouted Harry."Come on now put some elbow grease in them!"

By this command we took one oar each and started to row the great weight of the Mary-Anne seawards, this was what we were dreading. Conditions being so calm and with a slight westerly wind, we would have to row seawards until we could pick up enough breeze to fill the sails.

"Come on lads put some weight behind them oars." came the order again as Dick and I puffed and groaned with the weight of the fourteen foot oars.

We had just cleared the pier head when a slight breeze ran over us, filling the mainsail and relieving the weight from the oars, thank goodness for that I thought, lets just hope the breeze keeps up and freshens a bit more.

"Alright lads ship the oars," came the order from Harry who was relaxed in the stern holding the tiller and puffing away at his pipe.

Quickly we brought the oars inboard and secured them under the rail, the Mary-Anne heeled slightly over to starboard as the breeze freshened and filled the sails. Now clear of the shelter of land we would have enough wind to take us on the rest of our journey. Harry sat down on the after deck, and lighting his pipe again as it appeared to have gone out, puffed away, happily at the thought of a pleasant and calm trip, his red face glaring into the morning sun which had by now risen to it's full strength above the horizon.

"Looks like being a nice day lads, just enough wind to make the old girl move." Harry announced as he once more turned his head to the nor'east.

We had some six hours sailing to do before reaching the area where we intended to start fishing, which gave us a chance to have a welcome break. One thing was for sure, there'd be no rest once we started fishing.

Dick had slipped into the bilges and with his head resting on the nets had fallen asleep, probably from the affect of the ale the night before, more that the effort of the work we had done. I meanwhile leant over the bow and watched the sea as we gently and silently sailed seaward, hardly making a wave as the Mary-Anne's bows gracefully cut a path through the glassy surface.

Some score or so of ships were running up channel, every inch of sail set and just about making headway against the tide. Although the Mary-Anne was making way, it was slow, but these huge ships needed a bit more wind to push their great hulls through the water. Passing by the first ship, a Brigantine, called the 'Charles Henry' Harry laughingly, gave the crew on board her a bit of a sarcastic remark.

"Ahoy there...Charles Henry... If you throw me a line I'll give you a tow."

His face cracked with a sniggering grin as he slid back against the aft deck trying not to burst out laughing. Without any warning a shower of rotten oranges came flying down onto our deck, one of which caught Harry straight between the eyes. Angrily he jumped to his feet, waved his arms and fists at the men on board the Charles Henry and shouted.

"What's up with you lot, cant you take a bloody joke? If I was closer I'd….I'd…."

Suddenly Harry quietened down, he pushed the tiller hard over and the expression on his face turned from an angry red to a worried pale. A slight bump was felt beneath the Mary-Anne's keel, we had clipped the edge of a submerged sandbank, During the shouting and arguing the Brigantine had slowly altered course and forced us over to the edge of the Goodwins, poor old Harry was too busy gloating over his joke to notice what was happening. The channel was narrow here in the Gull stream, and mistakes could not be afforded.

"That was close." Shouted Harry as we pulled clear of the bank and ran astern of the Brigantine."Damned idiots nearly run us aground, what are you laughing at Tom? It isn't funny." He said as he slumped back against the tiller.

"Nothing Harry." I said still having a job to contain my laughter.

A loud cheer was coming from the Charles Henry, with one well built coloured chap leaning over the stern and shouting to us.

"Want a tow old man, or a few lessons in seamanship." He shouted to us as the rest of the ship's crew laughed even louder.

Harry wasn't amused at the outcome, and ignoring the insults being given him, he set about his course once more to the North sands head.

"You can shut up as well Tom, I don't want any funny remarks from you." he said, muttering under his embarrassment.

Once again on our course and leaving the ship astern of us, we settled back to the task in hand, still with the echoes of abuse and insults coming from the Charles Henry which was now well distant from us.

"Good job they weren't a few more yards inside of us." Harry said sort of cunningly." They would have struck the bank and gone aground, and then we would have seen who had the last laugh."

Harry turned around and took a last look at the ship as she slowly left us astern of her, sniggering at his ill intended thought.

"Call me names would they, you'll see mates, you will be sorry one day, you'll need old Harry here. You'll see. ."He shouted to them.

All through this excitement, Dick had been lying on the deck fast asleep, nothing had stirred him a bit.

"Lazy little beggar, can't even keep his eyes open to give me some support." Said Harry as he starred at Dick

We approached the North Goodwin lightship, and came up on her starboard side, hailed the crew and exchanged greetings, checking if they were alright and to ask if any supplies were needed, then we continued to sail towards the grounds that we had decided to fish.

A light westerly breeze now took us steadily eastwards, hardly making any way we slid through the unbroken sea as silently as a ghost, undisturbed surface cracking gently as the Mary-Anne's bows forced it apart. It took less than an hour to reach the grounds where Harry had decided to shoot the fleet of mackerel nets. These nets to enlighten you again, were similar to the herring nets we used, but with a slightly larger mesh, some mile and a half of drift net suspended from the from the surface by buoys that were tied every four fathoms, The depth of the nets was set at four fathoms, allowing any ship that should happen to pass over them, to do so in safety, without fouling the nets.

"Drop the main sail." Harry ordered, as he started to lower the mizzen sail.

Dick, who was now awake and conscious again, untied the halyard whilst I released the sheet that secured the mainsail, we lowered the huge sail down and neatly rolled it up and stowed it along the inner gunwale of the starboard beam out of the way of the nets, which we were going to shoot over the port side.

Slowly the Mary-Anne lost her head way and gracefully came to a halt, rolling gently in the calm sea. The small single cylinder petrol engine that was installed in the Mary-Anne was started, and the Mary-Anne's head was turned to the west, the engine put in astern gear and all was ready. Slowly the Mary-Anne started to go astern; the engine was just powerful enough to give her enough way to let us shoot the nets, which was all that was required, far easier than shooting under sail.

"Let Go!" Came the order from Harry who was standing in the stern, with a long oar in each hand which he was dabbling the water with, in order to control the boat and to hold her on a straight course.

Instantly Dick threw the first buoy over board, followed by the tall dhan with its bright red flag trailing from the top of the long pole. The strain came onto the ground rope, over the side I threw it, then yard by yard Dick and I steadily threw the nets overboard as the Mary-Anne slowly made her way stern first to seaward, dozens of buoys started bobbing about ahead of us as the nets settled to their pull, drawing out in a straight line as far as the eye could see.

"That's the last one Harry." Dick's voice bellowed over the noise of the petrol engine.

Harry pulled the long oars aboard and stowed them under the thwarts out of the way, turned off the engine and hoisted the large mizzen sail, this would keep the Mary-Anne's head into the wind and hold the nets out straight with a constant taughtness being put on the nets as the breeze tried to blow the boat out to sea. Dick had meanwhile secured the swing rope on the main mast and the Mary-Anne settled to the long drift ahead.

"All fast and secure here Harry." said Dick as he turned and sat down on the forward thwart, puffing and panting like an old man.

The gentle breeze filled the mizzen sail and it flapped noisily against the mast, the swing rope connecting us to the nets tightened slightly, as steadily the strain of the Mary-Anne pulling against it put her head into the breeze. It was now going to be around seven hours before hauling would commence, the Mary-Anne along with her mile and a half of nets would drift helplessly along with the tide, waiting for the mackerel to come along and swim into them. Sometimes we were lucky enough to find a shoal as soon as the nets were shot, and could haul straight back, this was always wished for, but normally we would continue drifting with the tide for several hours, eventually waiting for darkness to fall, when the mackerel would come up off the bottom and swim into the nets.

Some two miles further out to sea there were several French fishing boats working, fishing for mackerel the same as us, with drift nets, these French fishermen were common visitors along this part of the coast during the mackerel season, France being only a score or so miles distant. They were very handy fishermen to have about at times as well, as many a good catch has been sold to them at a better price than we could get at home. Excepting the odd one that always tried to take advantage of an easy cargo and a quick profit.

Harry too had noticed the activity of the Frenchmen, and was staring hard to get an idea of what was happening out there to seaward of us.

"Looks like those Frenchmen might have found a bit of fish lads." Harry said turning for a moment to look at us. "They don't hang around together like that for nothing."

"Aye it could be so Harry." I answered."Let's hope we find plenty as well."

We all settled back and put our feet up on the thwarts, it was going to be a long wait until dark by the looks of things, before we would start hauling. Harry sat stretched along the after thwart, his head staring constantly out towards the Frenchmen, hardly blinking an eyelid, and saying nothing. No telling what he was scheming in that brain of his, there was always something being planned.

Several sailing vessels had come our way and passed, without incident over the top of the nets clearing the headline easily, as we had set them below the depth drawn by the average ship. It was about an hour before dusk, when Harry suddenly jumped to his feet, put his hand over his eyes to stop the glare of the sun which was reflecting off the water, and stared at something away out on our beam.

"Looks like we have company lads,." he said, pointing out to sea.

Dick and I pulled ourselves together and looked around in the direction that Harry was pointing. Sure enough, coming in under full sail towards us was one of the French fishing vessels.

"I wonder what he's after?" said Harry. ."He seems to be in a mighty hurry."

Within ten minutes the Frenchman had lowered his sail and pulled alongside us, her hull towering well above our gunwales. These French fishing vessels were very large, as they were built to work in the worst possible weather far out in the North Sea.

"Hello there mon ami." shouted one of the Frenchmen. "Have you caught any fish yet monsieur?"

Harry trying to look a hard man pulled his chest in and replied in a gruff voice.

"No, not yet mates, we haven't had a haul yet, it's our first drift."

"Ah good monsieur, we have plenty of horse mackerel, no mackerel though. If you get plenty of mackerel or horse mackerel we will buy them from you monsieur. We will give you a good price. Said the Frenchman.

Old Harry looked the Frenchman straight in the eyes and grinned.

"Have you got plenty of money mates, if we get plenty of mackerel we will sell them to you, ok!"

A snigger ran through Harry's voice again, he was, in his own way taking the micky out of the way the Frenchman spoke.

"Ok monsieur, we go back to fishing now, you have fish you want to sell, you come find me, I buy, qui?"

"Aye matey, no problem we'll come and find you, we take plenty of money from you Frenchy, old Harry here catch plenty fish later, see you then."

Harry sat back down in the stern again, as the French fishing boat made sail, and waving at us, they set course again back to the fishing grounds where the other French boats were working.

"Can't be doing very good out there can they lads? We'll see how we get on later." Harry said.

"What time do you plan on hauling in the gear Harry?" I asked.

Harry looked around, then stared in the direction of the nets, took off his cap and scratched his head. Then answered.

"It will be dark in about half an hour; we'll start one hour after dark lads, give the mackerel time to rise from the bottom. It should be an easy haul tonight, there's no wind is there?"

I acknowledged Harry's orders and set about lighting the paraffin lamps, then carefully hauled them up the mast head, this would not only let other shipping know where we were, and stop us being run down in the dark by some large sailing ship passing our way, but also give a bit of light on deck to work with when we started hauling the gear.

Our oilskins were taken out of the forward locker and readily put on, these would stop us getting soaking wet as we hauled the nets, it's surprising how much water a net can hold when hauling, without oilskins we'd be soaked in no time.

"All right lads,." came the order from Harry who was standing astern all dressed and ready to haul, his pipe lit and hanging down from his bottom lip. ."Lets start hauling and see how we've got on, it's dark enough now."

Dick commenced hauling in on the swing rope, pulling the Mary-Anne up to the beginning of the nets; he hauled the first buoy aboard and waited for me to pull the ground rope up.

"I'm ready when you are Dick." I said as I started to pull the ground rope in." All clear Harry."

Harry took one of the large oars and placed it into the rowlock aft, this would be used to control the way the Mary-Anne laid as we hauled the nets. It would be used to stop her running over the top of the nets as there wasn't enough wind to keep us blown clear, a couple of gentle pulls on the oar would be enough to hold her off.

Hauling in the mile and a half of nets began. Yard after yard came aboard, without a single mackerel, but: to our surprise we had found what seemed to be an endless shoal of horse mackerel. These were no good at all on the English market, as people in England didn't eat them. But in France they were considered a delicacy.

"Look Harry! All horse mackerel." I said, momentarily glancing astern at Harry.

"Aye, no wonder the old Frenchy came and offered to buy our catch from us. He can have them too, they're no good to us." Harry commented.

We continued to haul without any problems for the next two hours, horse mackerel coming over the rail in their hundreds, with only the odd mackerel scattered amongst them.

."There it is Tom!" Dick eagerly shouted as he leant over the side and grabbed the dhan.

"Thank heavens for that." I said as I pulled the last bit of the ground rope aboard and fell against the side of the boat almost exhausted.

Although there was no wind, and hauling had been quite easy, pulling in a mile and a half of net full of fish was enough to make anyone's arms ache to dropping point.

"We've done well with horses lads haven't we? Come on; let's get these fish cleared from the nets and back over the side. We might find some mackerel on the dark drift, look lively now." Harry said as he started to help shake out the nets.

The task now was to shake out the horse mackerel, and as we cleared the nets, to re-shoot them over the other side, letting the light breeze blow the Mary-Anne steadily out to sea. As we payed the nets overboard each horsey was shaken out, Harry was boxing up whilst Dick and I again were lumbered with the arduous task of shaking out, good old Harry, always got the easy job but then I suppose that's what skippers were for.

Almost two hours had passed by when the last bit of the net was cleared of its catch and passed away over the side into the dark, followed closely by the swing rope. All secured again we helped Harry to box up the last of the horses and stow them across our midships, just astern of where the nets would be stowed when we hauled again later. This kept the Mary-Anne in good trim and made sure she wouldn't lie wrong in the water, which could cause her stability to be threatened if the wind should rise.

"Not a bad catch lads, about four hundred stone of horses, pity they weren't mackerel though. Still we can sell them to the Frenchies in the morning. You can get your heads down for a couple of hours now if you like, I'll keep watch." Harry said as he turned his head seaward and proceed to light his pipe.

We all settled down on the deck and covered ourselves with the large mainsail, the lights blazed on the main mast above us, illuminating our deck and its cargo, there would be time now for about five hours sleep until daylight started to break, every bit of which would be taken advantage of, that's if all went well and no ships came running on our course. All was quiet, with just the gentle lapping of the water breaking on the Mary-Anne's side disturbing the stillness of the night, I don't remember much more until Harry's voice woke me suddenly, breaking the peace and tranquility of the dream I was embraced in.

"Come on you lazy lot of land lubbers, time to haul." Shouted Harry as loud as he could, as if we were miles away and not just under his chin.

With a start Dick and I jumped dazedly to our feet, not quite awake and still somewhat confused as to where we were. The sea was still flat calm, with hardly a ripple to be seen anywhere, it was a beautiful summer's morning, damp but mild, calm, still and uncanny. The sun was just rising over the horizon, deep red with a fierce look to it, colouring the white fluffy clouds with a deep crimson glow.

Wiping the sleep from my eyes, I looked around; Harry was standing looking at the sun rise, still puffing away on his pipe, letting out large plumes of smoke which hung in the still air above his head. He was in deep concentration, only breaking away from his thoughts for a moment as my eyes caught his attention.

"Good morning Tom, it doesn't look good, does it? Harry remarked, as once more he turned to view the sun rise.

To the west, over our bows could be seen the buoys, trailing away into the distance as far away as the eye could see, bobbing gracefully up and down as the gentle swell moved them in the calm of the morning, to the east was a deep red crimson sky, the likes of which we had seen many time before, a for runner to something none of us wanted to be caught in.

"What do you recon Harry?" I asked, as he ventured to place the long oar once more in the rowlock.

"It doesn't look good at all Tom, I've seen this type of sunrise and sky before, as well you have, normally leads to a blow from the sou'east. It won't be long before it's upon us I recon." Harry said banging the last of the tobacco from his pipe, and then placing the pipe back in his pocket.

"Aye Harry, I think you might be right there, she's sure got the makings of a blow about her this morning." I replied.

By now Dick, after washing his face in the cool sea, had become aware that he was again in the land of the living.

"What's up, who's blowing hard, where's that...where?" He exclaimed still a bit confused.

"Nothing Dick." I answered. ."Harry and I were just saying that it looked like there's a blow from the sou'east on the way."

"Oh that's all, is it?" he mumbled as his voice disappeared within his oilskin, which with much effort he was trying to get into as he pulled it over his head.

"When you are ready lads, we'll start hauling." Harry said, as he slackened the mizzen sheet.

Dick, now in his oilskin began hauling on the swing rope, at once the Mary-Anne responded and drew closer to the nets, hardly disturbing the surface of the calm sea as she moved forward.

"There you are Tom, grab a hold." Dick said as he passed the leadline over to me and hauling commenced.

Slowly the nets came over the rail and inboard. Glittering in the morning sun as the water droplets fell from the meshes to the deck below. The nets were shining with patches of what looked like crimson embers of coal falling out of a fire, as the shapes of fish could be seen covering their surface.

"Looks like we've found the mackerel this time Harry; it's a good sign isn't it?" I remarked loudly.

Sure enough we had found a good haul of mackerel, thousands of them, from the top to the bottom of the net, there was hardly a mesh empty, yard after yard came aboard, stone after stone of fish, filling the Mary-Anne's hold. A short break came when two of the nets hauled aboard were completely empty, then again hundreds of mackerel, every net that came aboard was glistening with its immense catch of fish, putting a lot of weight in the Mary-Anne, and sitting her lower and lower in the water. She was a good boat for carrying a heavy cargo, but this was beginning to look a bit too much for her.

"Doesn't look like we will be able to carry this load Harry; she's getting rather low in the water now." I said a bit concerned.

"Ah! You panic to much Tom, we wont sink the old girl, until the waters level with the gunwales, that's the boat for those who are wondering what the old girl is, besides, we've got all those horse mackerel to unload onto the Frenchman yet, that will give us a bit more freeboard and some extra room. Keep hauling lads."

As we had been hauling, Harry had been busy scratching around in the after locker, mumbling and groaning to himself.

"Got it." came a sudden remark from the stern as he answered himself.

The next instant there was a bang, followed sharply by a roar. Harry had let off a white flare, which was glaring brightly against the red sky, high above us.

"That will do the trick." He muttered to himself again as he closed the door on the aft locker.

"What have you sent a flare up for Harry?" I asked him," There's no problem is there?"

"Look Tom, you have still got ten nets to haul yet, if they keep coming aboard like they are with that amount of fish we won't be able to carry them. I don't like shaking good fish back over the side."

"No I suppose we won't be able to carry them all, but why set off the flare? We're not in trouble."

"Look out to the east you two, can you see them?" Harry said pointing out in the direction of some boats.

We stopped hauling and turned our heads to the east, sure enough we saw what Harry was watching. A flotilla of French fishing boats, all heading towards France and home.

"See them Frenchies going home? We have fish to sell and won't catch them up loaded like we are, The Frenchies know what a white flare is for, so it's my guess that one of them might alter course and come over to us. You get back to your hauling now. Snap to it." Harry said

Sure enough, it wasn't long before a French boat started bearing down on us, moving slowly in the breeze, which by now had started to freshen from the sou'east as daylight was coming in. Another two nets hauled aboard saw the Frenchman haul up alongside us.

"Good morning monsieur, what is your problem?" asked the Frenchman.

"Good morning matey, we have some very good horse mackerel for sale here, good size fish. Do you want to buy some?" Harry asked the Frenchman that was trying his best to communicate in our language.

"Qui monsieur, how many have you got that you want to sell me; it looks like you are nearly sinking with too much fish, eh! And still nets to haul, you have a big problem monsieur." The Frenchy cunningly commented.

"I think there should be about two hundred stone of horse mackerel matey, what price are you paying?" asked Harry again.

"Ah monsieur! We think looking at your boat that you have no more room for fish eh! Still have more nets in the water too, how are you going to carry all that weight monsieur? It looks to us that you need to sell the horse mackerel to make some room for the nets you still have to haul. Yes monsieur?" laughed the Frenchman.

Harry went deathly quiet for a moment, watching the Frenchmen as they laughed amongst themselves. He was stuck for an answer, and knew quite well the position we were in. It was sell the fish or throw them back in the sea to make room for the proper mackerel. The Frenchmen knew this.

."Monsieur! We will give you three English pennies for each stone of fish you want to sell us. A good price, yes?" shouted the Frenchman to Harry.

"Not so long as my names Harry, you robbing bounders, they are worth at least sixpence a stone, and I'll throw in the boxes for nothing." Harry replied. Keep hauling you two." He shouted in an angry voice to Dick and I as he turned waving his hands in the air.

We started to haul once more, with the Mary-Anne wallowing heavily in the steadily rising sea, the weight was becoming too much for her. If Harry didn't unload some of our weight we were going to go straight to the bottom.

"Harry!" I said in a quiet voice. ."If you want to keep our mackerel catch, which will fetch far more than the horse mackerel, then you will have to throw the horse mackerel over the side. The Mary-Anne can't carry all the weight, and we'll sink for sure, better three pence than nothing Harry." I said ducking my head down as I half expected a mackerel to come flying in my direction.

."Aye, I know that Tom, but three pence a stone is daylight robbery. Isn't it?" remarked Harry again. ."Anyway, you get on with your job and leave me to do the bartering, damned interfering scallywag."

"I know Harry, but it's still a few pounds extra in our pockets, better than dumping them. We've had the trouble of catching them and shaking out, besides if you don't want them, Dick and I will sell them to the Frenchies." I said in a gruff voice, not too pleased at his decision.

Whilst all this was going on, the Frenchmen had hoisted their sails and were preparing to leave, obviously thinking that they were wasting their time trying to barter with Harry.

"Auvoir monsieur, bon voyage." They shouted as the wind filled their sails, and their boat heeled over to the strain.

They were going to leave alright, and knew if Harry didn't accept their offer of three pence a stone he would have to throw his catch away. Harry by now was steaming mad and redder in the face than I had ever seen him before, blending in with the morning sky as if he were part of it.

"Rotten robbing lot of frogs." He angrily muttered. ."Ok Frenchy, you come back and I will sell my fish for three pence a stone, no boxes though, come on you bounders, come and get them." He shouted, as he waved his arms at the French boat.

The French boat, hearing Harry shouting at them, put about and once again came alongside, with the Frenchmen laughing and taking the micky out of us. What they were saying I had no idea, I couldn't understand a word, but they obviously thought it was funny.

"Tom! You and Dick continue hauling; I'll pass the fish over to the Frenchmen, take it steady now."

We kept a slow haul going whilst Harry proceeded with the job of trans shipping our boxes of horse mackerel over to the French fishing boat, some foul language was coming from his direction at times as he complained about the Frenchies not grabbing the box, thus some of the fish fell in the sea, making our stoneage drop by a couple of pence. He was a tight chap when it came to doing business, but an excellent fisherman.

The last four nets to come aboard were a disappointment and very unusual, as they contained no less than a sprinkling of mackerel, not enough to fill a box, the fish had not swum into these, it seemed that the nets in the deeper water had done far better. A good thing really, as any more weight would have put us in a perilous position, so far off shore and the Goodwins to pass over on our way home.

Harry had now finished passing the boxes of horse mackerel to the French boat, and had been paid off in English money, something he insisted on as French money was no good to us. Dick and I slumped down on top of the nets totally exhausted, only too pleased of a rest now that the nets were aboard and we were finished until we set foot on the beach, then we would have the task of shaking out and boxing up. The Frenchmen set sail and went about their way, all sail hoisted and bows turned towards France.

"Bon voyage monsieur, good fishing next time you go to sea, we will see you again some day perhaps." Came the distant cry from their boat as it rapidly left us astern.

"They had us over a barrel didn't they lads, couldn't do much else could we? Still I suppose three pence a stone is better than nothing eh!" said Harry as he pushed the last of the money inside his trouser pockets.

Poor old Harry, he never liked being taken advantage of, but what else could he do, the Mary-Anne couldn't take any more weight of fish aboard, and she would run under as soon as we made sail. Dick and I kept quiet until Harry had calmed down a bit, thus avoiding raising his already bad temper which was on a knife edge. Harry sat on the aft thwart again and pulled the money out from his pocket , counting it carefully, and then a beam of light came across his angry face, followed by a huge grin, suddenly he jumped to his feet grinning and laughing with delight, this was a rather quick turn around, what had he found so amusing?

.Those stupid Frenchies have paid us five pounds too much lads, that will teach them to be so darn clever. Won't it lads?" He said laughing even louder.

This had brought a better situation to Harry, as he had got one over on the Frenchies, and now he was not feeling so embarrassed by losing his bargaining power, he laughed at his fortune until he was almost overcome by exhaustion.

By now the wind had freshened to a very stiff blow, the sea was covered in white crested waves, and a heavier swell was running beneath our keel. Dick and I had been grateful of a rest while Harry indulged himself in his prosperity; we had to make a start for home before the weather became too bad.

."What are we going to do Harry?" I asked calmly,." the winds freshening, and we have a long way to go to reach the beach."

"Aye I know Tom. It certainly looks like the winds on its way, I was going to have another shoot to try and fill that hole we have in the well,." he said jokingly. ."Never mind lads, lets get the old girl under way before it blows hard, hoist the jib and main you two, come on now, we haven't got all day."

We hoisted the sails and secured the halyard and sheet, the wind instantly filled the huge canvas and spread it out taught, taking every crease and smoothing it as if the canvas had been ironed flat. Slowly the Mary-Anne responded to the pull of the wind in the great canvas, and started making way heavily with a huge bow wave preceding her. She was laden with so much fish that her bows were only a couple of feet out of the water now she was under way. With the following sea she was rather a job to handle and Harry would have to put all his experience in seamanship to get her home without driving her under. There was more weight of fish in her than we thought.

Like an overloaded barge, she thrust herself forward before the wind, cutting the sea into two great waves which ran either side of her bows, hardly rolling or pitching, just lying heavily in the water, shaking herself as she rose on a swell, then wallowing in the trough as if she didn't want to rise again.

The wind by now had freshened to almost a full gale the sea had become heavier, although not overpowering as yet, the swells never made so much height on a SE wind for some reason, just a lot of short seas with broken tops, these were just as dangerous for a boat in our condition.. Two reefs were taken in on the mainsail slowing the Mary-Anne down, as she was running too fast before the wind and sea, and could quite easily run under should she catch a wave wrong and swing broadside on to the sea.

Within an hour we hauled up upon the port side of the North Goodwin lightship which was making heavy work of riding out the sea, rolling heavily in the swell as it broached her beam on, not a very comfortable position for the crew members on board.

Heavy seas were now breaking over the Goodwin Sands, and there was no chance of running over them and taking a short route as we usually did at high water, so it was decided to be a better option to run for Ramsgate harbour. A wise decision, if we had turned towards Deal beach we would have to sail beam on to the sea and wind, the Mary-Anne couldn't survive this as she was far to low in the water, heading for Ramsgate would at least keep us on a following sea. It would be easier to shake the catch out on Deal beach than in the harbour, but the other problem was also beaching the Mary-Anne, with a lot of swell running ashore, and the weight in her, she was sure to fill on hitting the beach, this would make it impossible to draw her clear of the surf and possibly cause much damage, so Ramsgate it was.

A heavy and wet trip across the North Brake sands saw us standing off Ramsgate harbour, the piers of which were being buffeted by huge waves lifting high into the air, drenching the whole town within it. It didn't seem this bad to us whilst we were sailing in, but looking at the harbour, well it didn't look very nice.

"It's going to be a bit of a job getting in lads, there's a lot of sea running in the harbour entrance, hang on tight now Harry." said, as he put the tiller hard over.

Harry turned the Mary-Anne's head towards the entrance, payed out some of the main sheet to stop the Mary-Anne heeling over too much as we now had to run beam on to the wind and then stood firm, grasping the tiller tightly with both hands. On went the Mary-Anne, gathering speed as she ran beam on to the wind, the sea was running up over her bows as she sped forward and thrust her head down. A giant sea hit us astern, lifting her up and throwing her heavy hull towards the harbour wall. Harry instantly pushed the tiller hard over, struggling to bring the Mary-Anne back on course, over she went, almost on her beam, with water cascading inboard in the gallons. We were unable to get to the pump to try and relieve her of the added burden of the extra weight the water had put within her hull, she couldn't survive this for long.

The sea was now starting to pour over her gunwales as she heeled over too far, Harry had to keep way on otherwise we would be thrown onto the harbour wall and be dashed to pieces, so there was no choice, Dick and I frantically grabbed the buckets and started bailing her out, it would stop her sinking at least. Luck had it though, another huge wave picked her up astern and with terrific speed she rode rapidly forward, just suspended by her amidships, going so fast that the stern and bow were suspended in the air, so fast in fact that the sea rushed away from her and was unable to come inboard, we had enough on board anyway, a few more gallons and we would surely be done for. In she went, straight through the entrance, past the pier head and on into the calmer water inside into the protection of the high walls, watched by dozens of spectators that were lining the pier, waiting for us to have a mishap.. We had made it, though only just, she stood but two planks out of the water, a near thing as one more good wave would have sent her to the bottom, and most likely us with her.

"That was a close thing lads; I thought we were going to be a goner there. Get ready to come alongside." Harry said.

Harry lowered the mizzen whilst Dick and I lowered the mainsail, leaving just the jib running. Slowly the Mary-Anne came alongside the harbour wall.

"Good lads, get the mooring ropes ashore and tie her off, Hurry up now before the wind blows her away from the wall." Harry shouted.

Dick climbed the steep iron steps that were hanging down the side of the harbour wall, taking with him the mooring ropes. Gaining the top and heaving himself over onto the safety of the wall he set about tying the ropes around the bollards that were set in the wall at sixty foot intervals.

"All fast and secure up here Tom." He shouted as he leaned over the top of the wall.

"Alright Dick." I replied as I pulled in the slack, passing one rope to Harry in the stern and fastening the other one around the cleat on the Mary-Anne's bows.

."All secure up forward Harry." I said as I started taking off my oilskins.

"Well Tom! That was an experience, wasn't it, very lucky there, we were. Still we are safe now."

"Yes Harry, a bit scary, a near thing, too close for my comfort. I though we were going to lose her and meet Davy Jones today. I'm certainly glad to be in here, safe and sound." I replied.

The wind was now blowing a full gale from the sou'east, just as we expected it to do, after the warning in the red morning sky. There was no chance of returning to Deal beach in these conditions.

"Well lads1" Said Harry as Dick jumped back aboard. ."We'll get the nets shook out, sell the catch here, and go and get a well earned pint. We might have to stay in the inn for a couple of days though, while this storm blows itself out." Harry said.

With some help from a couple of local men and their boat, we commenced the task of shaking out the mackerel. Meanwhile, in all the excitement, a large crowd had gathered on the harbour wall above us, all pointing and shouting out.

"What's going on up there?" Harry asked Dick as he had just come down the ladder.

"A large ship Harry, Looks like she's driving ashore on the sands just the other side of the harbour wall." Dick replied.

Harry immediately seeing a chance of a few extra shillings turned to one of the Ramsgate men that were helping us and asked which boat was the best in the harbour suited for a rescue job.

"What for?" one of the men asked.

"Why to go and rescue them poor souls on that ship that they say is going ashore matey. Who wants to come with me?" He replied sternfully.

Volunteers were plentiful, and with Harry in charge they manned a local trawler, in the hopes of aiding the ill fated ship.

The harbour entrance had become a mass of heaving, seething water, not a place where any small boat was cut out to be, but gallantly, the small vessel manned by some four oars each side, pulled towards the entrance of the harbour, on the hopes of gaining access to the wild open sea and the wreck beyond.

With the ebb tide now running hard, and sou'east wind blowing a full gale it would be totally useless in trying to hoist the sail, this would only impair the efforts of those trying to escape the turbulence being caused by the back splash from the two harbour walls. Mizzen only set, in order to keep the boat's head to wind, the boat and its crew of volunteers entered the turbulent seas at the entrance to the harbour. One minute they were high in the air, the next they had dropped in the trough of the following wave and disappeared out of sight. Spectators watching from the safety of the harbour wall with fear as the volunteer's boat came that close to the harbour wall, that we all thought she was going to be smashed to pieces. Pulling on the oars with every ounce of energy in their bodies the volunteers tried their hardest to gain a passage to the open sea beyond the harbour. It seemed effortless, as every sea that came in just pushed them back to where they had started. I mention the boat as being small, but she was in fact thirty feet in length, small by comparison to some fishing boats, but being handled by oar, she was a large craft to move.

I knew that Harry being skipper of the rescue boat would make the whole difference, as he was one that was very reluctant to give in once he had started on a mission.

Dick and I climbed the steep ladder that hung against the harbour wall, on reaching the top of the wall we positioned ourselves so that we had a full view of what was happening, not only with the rescue boat, but the distressed ship as well. Not that we could give any assistance if we had to, that was impossible in these conditions.

"They will never make it Dick." I said desperately. ."No boat can live through that, look at those seas coming in, they'll founder for sure."

Dick turned to me nodding and agreed solemnly, that it would be a miracle if they came through the rescue in one piece. Our attentions were distracted momentarily by the ship that was in danger. Hundreds of people had gathered on the beach just to the north of the wall, covering the sand like ants.

"She's hard and fast ashore now Tom." Dick said, as he wiped the spray out of his eyes.

Sure enough, during the commotion and concern for Harry and his volunteers in the rescue boat, we had all but forgotten about the ship that they were desperately trying to go and help. She was hard aground and had started to break up fast in the pounding seas, there was nothing anyone could do to help from the seaward now, any boat attempting to go alongside would just end up with the same fate, being cast upon the beach and smashed to pieces.

Quickly Dick and I rushed out to the end of the harbour wall, getting a good soaking as large seas broke against its outer side and rushed high into the air and shoreward's,. Frantically we waved and signaled to the crew in the rescue boat that was still being tossed about below us and hardly making any way at all. Dick was shouting at the top of his voice, but it was useless, they couldn't hear us over the roar of the sea and wind. I was waving, along with the harbour master, who by this time had come out of his office to give a hand in trying to attract the attention of the boat's crew. Harry's face, red from the stinging spray suddenly looked up towards us, he, if anyone would know what we were trying to say, we Deal boatmen had signals for most events that took place. I waved frantically again, telling him it was no use continuing. The message was understood, the oars suddenly stopped beating the sea, and the boat glided rapidly back through the harbour entrance, being pushed by the strong wind and following sea, it seemed as though the boat was almost pleased to be back, and that the crew aboard her had decided to abandon their fruitless task.

Dick and I went over to where the boat had berthed, and found the several men that were manning her, had already disembarked and were standing on the steps, soaking wet from top to toe and looking quite glum.

"What's all the panic for Tom?" asked Harry as I approached him, gasping for every breath after running the length of the harbour wall.

I explained to Harry and the rest of the crew what had happened to the ship whilst they were trying to row out to it, telling them that she was rapidly going to pieces on the beach just over the wall where we were standing.

"Thanks Tom." Came the answer from one of the crew members. ."We just couldn't get enough power behind the oars to pull clear of the bar anyway, it was a hopeless task in that sea, still I suppose we tried our best." He said.

Harry and the men decided to go and get some dry clothes on as there was nothing much we could do now, one of the Ramsgate men from the mission had been watching all that was going on and came out well prepared with a dry set of clothing for each man. This they instantly changed into, shivering like wobbling jellies in the bitter cold wind.

Dick and I had two volunteers to help us finish shaking out the mackerel, so leaving the others to get changed into dry clothes; we went back to the Mary-Anne and continued with the task of shaking out the mackerel from our nets.

"When you have finished boxing up Tom, bring yourself and those two lads over to the pub, will you? We will have a couple of pints and get a warm up." Harry shouted to us as he and the others started to leave the harbour.

I acknowledged Harry's offer, although not a drinker, one wouldn't hurt on a day like this, besides the warm up alongside a nice log fire would be more than welcome.

Some two hours had passed by before Dick, myself and the two Ramsgate helpers had finished shaking out and boxing up the fish. The fish merchants had been contacted by Harry earlier, and were on the quay side loading up our catch. The Mary-Anne was washed down, sails were stowed and all made shipshape ready for her to set sail again as soon as conditions permitted it.

"Well that's about it." I said to the others as I washed the last of the mackerel scales from my hands. "I'll just check on the fish merchants, and then we'll be off for that hard earned pint of beer and a warm up."

We ascended the ladder and I took note from the main fish buyer who was waiting at the top of the steps for me, as to how much we had caught and what price was being paid for the fish. The four of us then strolled along the quay towards the ale house, staring at the people on the sand below on our right hand side, and the poor misfortunate vessel that had found her grief in such an embarrassing manner.

"I hope nobody's been drowned." I commented to the others. "It's a shame, a ship like that broken to pieces, a terrible waste of a good vessel."

We couldn't do anything for the ship or the poor souls that were on her, there were more than enough skilled helpers down there on the shore, as well as all the ordinary people that had turned out to volunteer their services, so we turned our heads, walked across the road and entered the ale house

****

Chapter 8

<u>The Trip to Lowestoft</u>

The evening in the tavern, although a welcome break from the terrible weather outside, wasn't my idea of spending a nice night by a warm fire. After all, I, unlike the others didn't indulge in drinking, don't get me wrong, I enjoyed the occasional pint, but for the life of me couldn't see how anyone could enjoy themselves by becoming drunk, and then flat broke the next day, and suffering from a splitting headache.

Sitting down next to Harry, I informed him what had taken place with the catch, where it had gone, and how much it had made, he didn't say much apart from a grunt coming from the inside of his glass, as he swallowed another mouthful of ale. By the short time he had been here he had become quite intoxicated, or rather the worse for wear. Other seamen were standing around the bar with pints in their hands, discussing the fate of the ship that had been driven ashore on the sands opposite the tavern, or what was left of the ship would be a more accurate description now. Dick was enjoying a few jugs of ale as well, this was an ideal situation for him, he loved his ale and nothing suited him better than to spend all day in a tavern drinking, so with no where else to go, I had no choice, but to take a glass of ale, sit by the fire and try and except the situation, anyway I would be out of here tomorrow if the weather eases, and would be sailing back to Deal hopefully.

Sitting beside Harry at the table we talked about the day's work that had just passed, and what we would do as soon as the weather abated, storms of this magnitude were very unusual and normally never lasted very long. The hours passed away more like minutes, with another glass of ale finding its way to my mouth, I was not used to drinking this ale, and it wasn't very long before my memory faded and I vaguely remember being sick, and then being sort of manhandled into a room where I was laid on a bed. Everything from then seems to be blank.

I woke up the following morning with one heck of a head ache, stumbling somewhat on my feet as I struggled from my bed and attempted to get dressed, never again, I said to myself as I fell clumsily onto the bed again, if this is what they call having a good time, I'll go without.

Bracing myself up and looking out of the window I could see that the wind had dropped and the sea was quite calm; a distinct contrast to what it had been like the night before. Good, I thought we should be sailing today back to Deal, so gathering myself together as best I could in the circumstances, I made my way down the twisting wooden stairs to the bar below, staring around a bit glassy eyed, I could see no one except a couple of people talking at the far end of the bar chatting over a glass of ale.

."Where's Harry?" I asked the bar woman, as I flopped over the bar, still a bit unsteady on my feet.

A pretty dark haired woman smiled at me from across the other side of the bar, and then moving towards me and putting her arm over my shoulder, quietly answered my question.

."Harry!" she said."Harry and Dick both left here at nine this morning my friend, they couldn't wake you up dear, tried hard they did, but you were out for the count."

."Have you any idea where they went my dear?" I asked her again, as I looked into her beautiful dark brown eyes.

."I don't know, they sailed just after nine this morning, the last time I saw of their boat it was making way out to the east. Harry told me to tell you he would see you back on Deal beach, that's if you sobered up enough."

."They sailed just after nine!" I exclaimed anxiously. ."What time is it now then?"

."It's just passed five in the afternoon Tom, You've certainly had a good sleep haven't you?" she answered as she ran her hand through my hair and caressed my face.

."Five in the afternoon. Why didn't somebody wake me? They will be home and finished by now." I replied, pulling myself away from her passionate grasp, not that I really wanted to, she had a touch like silk and it felt quite nice.

."We tried to wake you Tom, as I just said, but you must have had far too much to drink last night, you were dead to the world, we couldn't get a shuffle out of you, so we left you there to sleep it all out of your system." Answered the young woman, once again trying to passionately caress me.

I immediately thanked the young woman, pulled myself together lifted her arm from my shoulder, and left the tavern, making my way across the road to the harbour. Sure enough the Mary-Anne had gone, along with most of the other fishing boats that were moored up there.

The sea was flat calm again, as if nothing had ever happened it seemed like some sort of a dream. I looked over the other side of the harbour wall and realized that the events of the day before had been real enough, there was wreckage from the ship strewn from one end of the beach to the other, with the main part of her hulk still lying on the sand where she had struck, battered and broken into a pile of firewood, her sails and spars were hanging from the large exposed timbers that once held her frame together.

Pulling myself together, I paused to think what I was going to do next. I had no money on me, so couldn't take a coach to Deal, all the other boats in the harbour had put to sea, so the chance of catching a run out to the fishing grounds where Harry would be working was out of the question. What was I going to do?

Wandering slowly along the harbour wall, with my head hanging down almost in my lap, I accidentally bumped into a tall red faced seaman, who, when I approached him, pulled me up sharp.

."Looking for a berth mate?" he said to me in a deep gruff voice.

."Why, er yes sir!" I answered in a sort of confused and unexpected way. I've missed my boat; she's gone to sea without me.

."That's not a problem is it mate?" he replied. ."Local lad are you: how well do you know the waters out here?"

."Aye, sort of local you might say, and I know the waters like the back of my hand sir, I've spent all my life so far out there. Why?" I answered.

."Well mate we are bound for Lowestoft and need a pilot, it seems all the pilots are also fishermen around these parts, and they have all gone to sea as one of their boats apparently had a good catch yesterday. There's no one left here to pilot our ship now. Would you like the job mate? The pays pretty good." He said to me.

I looked up into his face astonished at his request, at first not knowing what answer to give him, then without question replied to his demand.

."Why yes sir, I'll take it, certainly I'll take the job, what ship are you from?"

."She's the Dart, lying over there on the western arm; she's loaded and ready for sea."

I looked in the direction of the western arm that he was pointing, sure enough on the western arm lay the Barque, as smart a ship as ever I did see.

."Is that your ship sir? That Barque over there sir." I asked inquisitively.

."Yes mate lovely vessel isn't she? Come on then, I'll take you over to her."

We left the eastern arm and walked together around to the western arm, talking and exchanging views.

."Come on Tom, come aboard." He said as he started to climb down the slippery ladder that hung precariously against the wall.

I followed him down the steep ladder, and gaining the deck was greeted by the crew.

."Come on lads, this here is Tom our new pilot, we can set sail now, get to it, lets get her under way."

With much scuffling the crew started preparing the Dart for sea; meanwhile I was shown to my cabin, where I would spend my time off watch. After putting my small amount of gear in the cabin, I decided to have a quick look around the vessel before we sailed, just to get an idea where everything was and how the vessel was worked.

She was a smart ship, about one hundred and twenty feet long, bristling from stem to stern, and without a ropes end out of place. The captain's name was Joe, a quiet and mild mannered sort of chap that everyone seemed to like very much. During our voyage I never heard him shout once at his crew. After I had given the ship a good overhaul I made my way back to the upper deck, where Joe was waiting to give my orders

."Are you all set Tom? Grand little vessel isn't she was built this year?"

."I thought she looked a bit too well kept for an old vessel." I answered."Who's her owner?"

."The owner, that's I Tom, she's my vessel. I worked hard on the Australian routes running immigrants for several years, saved every penny and now I am the proud owner of the Dart you've had a look round Tom, come on I'll come with you and show you her parts again and put you in the picture as to her workings."

We wandered up and down her decks, with Joe hardly letting me get a word in. he sure was proud of the Dart who could blame him; she was a well built smart vessel.

."How's it going mate?" Joe shouted to the mate who was up aloft in the main rigging.

."She'll be ready in ten minutes or so Joe, we're almost done up here." the mate replied.

."Well Tom I hope your navigation is good, if we reach Lowestoft within the week there'll be a bonus in it for you."

."The winds off west Joe, with fair conditions, so it should be no problem, I'll go topside and get the shore crew ready."

With this I ascended the steep ladders on the quay wall and gave the gang of men that were waiting at the top, their orders. I had sailed large vessels from Ramsgate before, so knew the ropes as to say, and was fully confident of piloting the Dart to Lowestoft, in a strange sort of way I was almost looking forward to the trip. A bit of revenge on Harry I suppose, for deserting me in Ramsgate.

Lines were thrown down to the Dart, with four big burley men hanging on to each one, the other ends were secured to the stern and bow of the Dart, climbing back aboard and asking if all was ready, I gave the signal to cast off. Top sails were lowered, and at the same time the men on the quay started pulling the Dart towards the entrance, using the iron bollards on the quay to keep her in close to the west wall. Slowly she came round to the open entrance, the sea was almost calm except for the ripples caused by the tide running past the wall. The wind took the topsails, filling them lightly and causing the Dart to tug hard on the shore lines, around the bow went towards the open sea.

."Let go ashore,." I shouted as the wind started to take control of the Dart. ."Up foresails. Tighten in on the main sheets."

Taking over at the wheel I left the captain to give the command for the rest of the sails to be hoisted and set, he waited; he knew what I was going to do, on clearing the wall I altered tack; then the order came ."Hoist all sail."

With the light westerly breeze and an easterly flowing tide the Dart started moving faster to seaward, a graceful a vessel in her movements I had never been on a ship that responded to the helm so easily before.

."All clear Tom, what do you reckon of her?" said Joe peering through the wheel at me and grinning with pride.

."I'll say one thing Joe, she handles mighty well. Looks a picture from the shore I bet." I replied.

There were crowds watching from every point along the shore, many most probably never having seen a sailing ship before as it now being summer a lot of holiday makers had arrived in the lodging houses.

Heeling slightly we gathered way to around five knots, gracefully pulling towards the Kentish knock banks. Banks notorious for the destruction of many a good ship. The Kentish Knock lies in the middle of the entrance to the Thames estuary, along with several other large sand banks, once clear of these banks it would be all plain sailing until we reached Lowestoft.

."Have you done much piloting Tom?" asked Joe as he stared out to the breakers which were running across the semi-submerged banks.

."Yes, I've done quite a bit, had to rely on it at times when fishing was bad you know, us Deal men can do just about anything, we know the area like the back of our hands."

."Deal chap eh!" he replied."My Uncle is a Deal man, Harry Baily is his name, do you know him Tom? He Lived in Middle Street last time I saw him."

."Well blow me down, who'd of thought that? I live in Middle Street and my skipper, that's the skipper I usually sail with on the Mary-Anne, is Harry Baily. Wait till I tell him I sailed with one of his kin. Well I be blowed!"

We got talking of our families and the going on's in Deal, hardly realizing how quick the time had flown pass.

."Well there she is Joe the end of the knock banks. We've a clear run now until we fetch up on Lowestoft. Give the order to come round thirty points to the north."

."Haul in on the starboard sheets lads. That's the way; we're setting a course to the nor'ard now."

The crew rustled about without much more hesitation, each man knowing his own duty.

."You've got a fine crew there Joe." I commented, as I watched them handling the sheets and halyards without any commands from the mate.

."Aye they've been sailing with me a few years now, I couldn't get a better bunch of lads."

."All squared up now Tom how it is?" asked Joe as he stood proudly by my side with one hand on the wheel.

."There you are Joe clear of the sands; keep this course for the next eight hours, there's nothing to hurt now, I'm going below for a few hours sleep, its nearly nine o'clock and darks setting in already."

."Thanks Tom I'll shout you later." Answered Joe as he took full control of the Dart from me.

Joe put the mate on the wheel and gave him orders and a course to follow, then followed me below for a few hours sleep, leaving the stillness of the night above.

With the coming of day light I was awakened by a hot cup of tea brought into my cabin by a young boy of about ten.

."Here you are sir, a nice hot cup of tea for you." He said as he passed me the cup.

."Well thanks lad, certainly smells good, thank you very much, you must be the cabin boy I recon." I asked him.

."The captain's told me to tell you it's a fine sunny day aloft, with a light westerly breeze, we're eight miles from Lowestoft, and could you come and take over at the wheel please."

."Sure lad, tell the captain I'll be there directly, just give me a minute to get dressed."

I got dressed, and grabbing my tea took a mouthful. I quickly spluttered it over the deck."Core, that's flaming hot, burnt my flaming tongue!"

I wasn't used to hot tea like this; still it serves me right, I shouldn't have taken such a large swallow. Taking my mug with me I made my way aloft and to the stern where Joe was standing holding the wheel with one hand.

."Have a good night Tom?" he asked.

."Yes thanks Joe, flaming tea was hot though, burnt my tongue!"

Joe and the mate laughed.

."He makes a good brew does our boy, forgot to warn you. How is it not serious I hope?"

."No I'll survive Joe, don't worry, I'll just be a bit more cautious next time I take a mouthful of tea."

I glanced around at the sea; it was almost flat with just a light breeze pushing us through the water. The land was showing up clear some five miles to the west of us, and I could just see the entrance to Lowestoft harbour ahead.

."We should be there in about three hours with a bit of luck Joe; here I'll take the wheel now."

I moved over and took the wheel whilst still holding my mug of tea in the other hand.

."Fine day Joe, ideal sailing weather." I commented as I stared towards the land that was just visible ahead of us.

."Sure is Tom. It didn't take us long to get to Lowestoft did it? Thought it might have taken all of four days."

."No, only a day normally, we've done well though, she's a fine old vessel, the best I've had fortune to sail on for a long while, I've been on a few as well."

I settled down to steering the Dart to Lowestoft, running up along the inside of the sandbanks that lie to the south of the entrance. A following tide was giving us a further four knots, cutting our sailing time by half.

On approaching the harbour mouth we were greeted by one of the local boats again plying a pilot.

."Want a pilot in captain?" came a voice from the little boat below. ."Mighty dangerous entrance here yer know, best be safe."

I looked at Joe, and he seemed uneasy, turning to him I reassured him of my capabilities.

."Don't worry Joe, I know my way, been here dozens of times here watch this."

I leant over the rail and hailed the pilot that was in the small boat below us.

."What's up mates?" I shouted as their faces turned to my direction.

."It aint!" One of the men in the boat exclaimed, as he took another look."It's….its…. it sure is; it's that Deal lad Tom we won't get a days work here." He shouted.

."See you ashore lads." I remarked laughingly as the little boat left us and set a course back to Lowestoft.

."Well Joe what'll you think now, Do you recon I can take her in through the piers without a local pilot?" I asked Joe as he watched the small pilot boat pull away from the Dart's side.

."It seems you've been here before,." he said laughing ."Carry on then, I trust you."

The sheets were tightened in and the Dart's head brought round towards the entrance. The tide had slackened so it would be easy entering. Steadily she pulled towards the entrance, with no effort at all.

As we rounded the western wall, Joe gave orders for the sails to be dropped, ropes were thrown to the shore hands, and within minutes the Dart was resting alongside the harbour wall motionless.

."Well Tom thanks: we had a good trip, come below and I'll settle up with you."

I followed Joe below deck and into his cabin, taking a seat at the large wooden table that was sat in the middle of the small room.

."There you are Tom, fees, plus a two pounds bonus. How's that suit you?" Joe asked as he passed me the money.

."Thanks Joe that'll do fine, I'm very grateful to you, I'll get my things and be off now."

."Tom! Before you go, if you'd like to take it, I could find you a permanent berth aboard here, I could use your help, there are not many good seamen about these days you know."

I stopped for a minute thinking, a regular wage; well this was worth having, but no not me.

."Thanks all the same Joe, but you know us fishermen, we like the smell of fish around us. Thanks all the same."

."A pity Tom, we could use your skill and knowledge aboard here with us still if you change your mind we'll be here a couple of days loading, The Job's yours if you want it."

."Thanks Joe, I'll bear it in mind. I'll get my gear now and be off."

Collecting my small amount of gear, I left the Dart bidding her crew farewell, still somewhat contemplating the offer aboard her. No it's not me; I must get back to Deal.

."So long mates, see you again one day perhaps." I shouted as I stepped off the Darts deck onto the harbour wall.

Waving I left the Dart and her crew behind me, and made my way along the quay to the local ale house. Hopefully to try and get a berth aboard a trawler or barge sailing down the channel towards Deal and home again.

****

A Lugger under full sail

Chapter 9

The North Sea fishing grounds

The harbour at Lowestoft was a bustle of fishing boats, unloading catches, and preparing to go to sea, with fish carts traveling too and fro busily along it's length , each one full to overflowing with freshly caught fish which would be bound for some fishmonger's shop where they would grace the window until sold.

"Hey! Tom." My name was being shouted from across the way somewhere.

I paused for a moment, not quite sure if it was addressing me or someone else that was being beckoned.

"Hey! Tom." Came the cry again with an anxious tone to it.

Again the voice shouted my name. Turning and looking downward I saw a tall thin chap waving his arms at me to attract my attention. It couldn't be! I thought, but with a second glance, it was, it was Jimmy an old friend of mine.

"Jimmy how the devil are you old fellow? It's been a long time since I saw you in these parts, what are you up to these days?"

"My old pal Tom, well who'd of thought it! Fancy seeing you here."

Jimmy and I were fortunate or unfortunate as the case may be, to have met during a gale. He had the misfortune to be one of the crew of a brig, wrecked on the Goodwin Sands, from which, as it turned out I happened to be his rescuer. From that day on we became very good friends, but after his sailing on a packet to Australia a couple of years ago I had lost all trace of him.

"Old Jimmy, what a small world. I heard you'd gone to Australia. What are you doing here in Lowestoft and aboard a trawler too? Well I be blowed!"

"It's a long story Tom, come aboard, have a brew with me and I'll tell you all about it."

I descended the ladder down the harbour wall and joined Jimmy on deck. We greeted each other like brothers, hugging and shaking hands and with tears in both our eyes from the happiness we were in on our reunion.

"It's good to see you again Jimmy, I've wondered many times how you were getting on in Australia; it seems you changed your mind though otherwise you wouldn't be here."

"Aye, well not just changed my mind Tom, I kind of had no choice, you see, the packet ship I was sailing on met the same fate as the ship you saved me from, a stroke of bad luck I guess."

"Oh! How's that Jimmy? I'm sorry to hear the bad news, what happened?"

"Aye well after leaving you in Deal I sailed for Australia on the packet as crew, as you know."

"Aye I know that Jimmy, I remember you leaving that day, it stuck in my mind for weeks."

"Well on reaching the shoals off Lowestoft we encountered a full gale from the nor'ard, not more than two days into the voyage."

"What happened Jimmy, go on?"

"Well Tom, we fought hard to make harbour here in Lowestoft; it was a terrific storm, we beat hard to make the harbour entrance but the sea was too much for the ship; she struck the banks and foundered."

"Bit of rotten luck Jimmy, two shipwrecks in a month. Did you all get saved?"

"Aye Tom, rough do though, if you look over the harbour wall you will see the wreck on the beach, we drove in at high tide, good job too. We all managed to scramble ashore at low water, as she was left her high and dry by then, but it put a stop on my going to Australia though."

"I'm sorry to hear that Jimmy, but what are you doing on a fishing boat? It's not like you; I thought you didn't like fishing."

"Well Tom, I didn't but a job came up, and not having any money left to buy a passage out, I had to find some work there's no other jobs here only fishing. So here I am, but this old girl is my own."

I drew back somewhat startled, and looked around at the vessel that Jimmy and I were standing on, and that he had apparently purchased.

"Your vessel Jimmy?" I exclaimed. ."You are of course kidding me on, aren't you?"

"That she is Tom; she's mine alright, you see, I shipped aboard her as crew when I first landed here, a job I suppose, I just wanted to earn enough to buy a passage out again. I didn't know a thing about fish or fishing, as you well know Tom. The skipper of her was a good sort; he kind of took me in; felt sorry for me I think in his own sort of way."

"So what happened Jimmy; how did you come about owning her then? Surely there's not that much money to be earn't in fishing in this area; is there?" I asked.

"Well Tom, I took the job he offered me and sailed with him on this boat, for some reason I seemed to be enjoying the job of catching fish for a living, and I got quite close to the old fella. When ashore he gave me a berth in his house Tom, as I had nowhere else to go, and we just became best mates, similar to you and I Tom. He treated me like his own son and I kind of respected him and looked on him as a father figure I suppose. His wife is one of the kindest women you could ever wish to know, she does everything for me. I recon as they had no children of their own, they kind of adopted me.

"Well the old chap taught me good and proper how to be a real fisherman, then one day he gave me command of his boat. I seem to have taken to the game now Tom, if you see what I mean."

"Aye, I sure do Jimmy, once a fisherman, always a fisherman, it sticks in your blood, keeps pulling you back to sea, there's no getting away once you have the calling." I said to Jimmy still inspecting the boat.

"Well!" Jimmy said sadfully. ."The old chap passed away five months ago, he just collapsed at the helm whilst we were out at sea fishing, and it broke my heart when that happened. I never had a real family before and didn't realize how much you could miss someone when they were gone. He left the boat to me, that's how I came to own her." Jimmy said.

"Well Jimmy, good luck to you, you deserve it, but what about the old chap's wife, how is she going to manage now, without him, and an income to live on?"

"She's fine Tom, I still live in her house, and she's very good to me, a grand old lady. I keep her in money though, wouldn't see her go without, besides after what they have done for me I consider it now to be my duty."

"So you intend to carry on fishing then Jimmy? Here in Lowestoft. Your Australian adventure is cancelled I presume?"

"That's about it Tom, here for good by the looks of things. I've a girl of my own now as well, local lass, we hope to get married this year some time. Aye its no moving now, Lowestoft is my home."

"I'll say one thing Jimmy; she's a fine fishing vessel, lovely lines to her."

"Aye that she has Tom, and she tows a treat in a breeze as well, handles like a dream. Anyway, what are you doing in these parts?"

I went on to explain what had happened to me on my last fishing trip on the Mary-Anne, and how I had sailed as a pilot on the Dart and ended up here, in Lowestoft.

"You see, that's how I came to be here Jimmy. I'm now looking for a berth or passage to take me back to Deal, I don't mind working my way home, so long as I can get near enough to get to Deal."

Jimmy went quiet for a moment, then turned and stared me straight in the eyes and said.

"What about sailing with me Tom? I could use a good hand. I'm not going fishing Deal way though; it's out to the Dogger Bank for fish. I've a good crew aboard here but could always do with another skillful hand that can take command in a situation, the pay's good Tom, and what do you say?"

"I don't know Jimmy." I said giving the matter my deepest consideration. "I'd like to get back home. Besides old Harry owes me my share of the last catch we had in the Mary-Anne yet, that should come to a pretty penny as well."

"Come on Tom, you've got nothing to lose have you, you can collect your money off Harry someday, I'm sure he will hold it for you, sign aboard here with me for a few trips. I tell you what, come back to the old house with me and have some dinner, take a bed for the night, then we can have a chat about the old times, and you can have a think on my offer."

"Alright Jimmy I'll join you for dinner and a nights rest, but I insist on paying my own way and board."

"Nonsense Tom the old girl will be more than pleased to have you and put you up for the night, we sail on the morning tide anyway."

"Thanks Jimmy, I'll come along and see how the other half live if nothing else. Lead the way."

"Come on then Tom, I'll take you back and you can meet mother, that's what we call her, come on, don't worry."

We climbed the ladder and looked over the top of the harbour wall. Jimmy pointed out the wreck of the Australian packet ship, which was lying beneath the wall on the sandy beach, then we slowly walked towards his house, talking about the old times we had spent together, and exchanging stories, until we came to a large beautiful house, standing in its own grounds, surrounded by a beautiful garden full of the most colourful and fragrant flowers of all varieties and types I had ever seen. The sight was stunning.

"Here we are Tom, this is my home." He said as he swung open the gate before me.

"This is massive Jimmy, surely this cannot be a fisherman's home, and you can't earn this sort of money in the fishing game."

"Aye it's my home Tom, and a beautiful place it is too, wait until you see the inside."

Entering the front gate and weaving through the flowers, which graced the path, we came to an archway covered with white roses, behind which was a concealed a large double fronted oak carved door.

"Come on Tom! In you come." Said Jimmy as he opened the door and went inside. ."Hello mother, I'm home."

I entered the house and shut the door behind me, glaring in amazement at the size of the room, with its old antique furniture, and walls all decorated with fine old oil paintings of vessels of all descriptions.

"Hello Jimmy dinners nearly ready." Came a gentle reply from the old lady.

Looking around to where the voice had come from, I saw a pretty little old lady of about sixty, dressed in a long black dress which was covered in embroidered flowers, a bonnet sat gracefully upon her head, with long dark shiny hair petruding from its sides, and a shawl graced her slender shoulders.

"This is Tom mother, an old friend of mine from Deal; he's a boatman there and saved my life a couple of years ago when I was shipwrecked on the Goodwin Sands. Can we find some extra dinner for him?"

"Tom!" she said moving closer to me. ."Come in Tom, take your coat off and have a seat at the dinner table, make yourself at home now, any friend of Jimmy's is welcome at my house."

"Thanks mother its very kind of you; I don't want to put you out in any way. You don't mind me calling you mother do you? Only Jimmy said that's what he calls you, thought it would be fitting to be polite."

"No, not at all Tom, you call me mother, everyone else does, and I'm used to it after all these years, now sit you down there while I dish up the dinner, there's always plenty to spare as I never know who's going to drop in. Young Jimmy is always bringing someone back home with him."

I sat down at the large dining table along with Jimmy, not quite knowing what to expect, glancing around at the paintings and carved furniture while I waited for the food to be served.

"Well Tom, what brings you to these parts then?" Asked mother as she placed a large plate of food in front of me.

My story of how I came to be in Lowestoft was once again repeated to mother, who listened interestingly to every word and detail.

"Come on now boys, eat your meal up before it gets cold, you can chat later, are you sailing with Jimmy in the morning Tom? He's a nice lad is Jimmy, he's like a son to me, I wouldn't know what to do without him. You'll have a good trip with Jimmy I'm sure, and when you come back if you have nowhere to go, there's always room here for one more, remember that Tom. Don't be shy in asking now."

I hardly had a chance to correct mother and let her know that I had not agreed to sail with Jimmy in the morning, but was just spending the night with him, when Jimmy suddenly replied.

"Yes old Tom's a great chap mother, we'll get on great together, and he'll enjoy his trip aboard the Jane-Ellen. You won't want to go home again, will you Tom?"

"Um, yes Jimmy." I answered somewhat surprised and not quite knowing whether or not I was to sail or return home, although it looked like my passage had already been booked to sail with Jimmy on the Jane-Ellen on the morning tide. ."Yes, I'm looking forward to sailing with Jimmy mother." I answered again.

It seemed that my mind had been made up by involuntary chatter. I was now sailing in the morning on board the Jane-Ellen with Jimmy and his crew, still I suppose it couldn't do me any harm; after all I was a fisherman at heart.

Dinner finished, we helped mother to wash and clear up, we then took a cup of tea, and made our way to a small table in the front garden where we sat and exchanged views.

It was a beautiful sunny afternoon; we talked about the sea and ships as would be expected from seamen, and enjoyed a very comfortable afternoons rest.

"Now then Tom, follow me and I'll show you to your room." Said mother as she got up from her seat.

Standing up I followed mother up the stairs, where she led me into a large room, again full of nautical items and antiques, with its windows facing the sea, out of which one could see every vessel passing up and down the channel.

"This was my husband's room Tom, I hope you like it, he spent hours in here watching the boats go to and fro."

"Thanks mother." I replied. ."It's beautiful; he must have been a wonderful character."

"He was Tom, one of the best. But the good Lord had better plans for him I guess, and I feel sure he's happy now." She answered with a tear in her eye.

"I'm sure he's happy mother, the good Lord's most likely got him fishing for all those angles up there in heaven." I said jokingly to cheer her up.

Mother left the room, shutting the door gently behind her. Poor old woman, she was still breaking her heart over losing her husband, poor old woman.

I moved over to the window and gazed through its opening, viewing the ships entering and leaving Lowestoft harbour, thinking what tomorrow was going to bring. Ah well! It's too late now; I had already told Jimmy I would sail with him, so was committed to go now. Still my money and hopefully berth aboard the Mary-Anne would be waiting for me when I returned to Deal. Harry wouldn't rob me.

"Tom! Tom!" Jimmy's voice bellowed up the stairs. ."Tom!" he shouted again.

I opened the door and looking over the banisters, answered him. ."Yes Jimmy, what is it?"

"I'm going for a jug of ale Tom; would you like to join me? Just one now."

"Aye that I will Jimmy, so long as its only one now. I'll be right with you."

I had in some sort of strange way enjoyed my last few beers at Ramsgate, although the result was a splitting headache the following morning, besides I couldn't really be unsociable, now. Descending the stairs I found Jimmy leaning against the banister waiting for me.

"Alright Tom, come on, it's only a short step up the road. See you later mother."

Closing the front door behind me, Jimmy and I set off to Jimmy's local ale house. It wasn't as far up the road as I thought, a quaint old wooden building, bursting with songs and laughter, from the occupants within, which were obviously having a whale of a time.

A loud cheer of welcome went up as we entered the door. Everyone was obviously pleased to see Jimmy, and I found out why later on. Jimmy had become in his short career as a fisherman, one of the top earners in the port, of which everyone sailing with him was classed as a millionaire.

"What will you have Tom?" Jimmy asked as he placed his elbow on the polished wooden bar.

."Just a beer please Jimmy, thank you."

We spent two enjoyable hours in the ale house, from which I was introduced to each and every man within, exchanging stories and escapades of the sea with them all, a well remembered night, and one which would not be forgotten. Unlike the boatmen at home in Deal, these men seemed more friendly, even sharing fishing grounds and boat catches with each other, so that no one came home with a bad catch, something the Deal men would never consider.

That night was one of the best I had been able to sleep through in ages, my dreams were directed towards Jimmy's boat and becoming a millionaire, until a voice woke me early in the morning.

"Tom are you awake? Tom, its time to get up lad." Said a quiet gentle voice.

Dazedly I stared through one eye; mother was standing at my bedside rocking me from side to side.

"Its time to get up Tom, Jimmy's downstairs waiting, and your breakfast is ready on the table."

"Good morning mother." I said as I struggled to join the world of the living. ."I'll be right down, thank you."

Dressing quickly I made my way down stairs to the dining room and took my place at the table. Jimmy was already sitting at the table having his breakfast, having been up some time.

"Good morning Tom! Grand morning out there this morning, get your breakfast mate, we've lots to do."

I had no sooner sat at the table and pulled my chair up, when mother came in with a large plate containing bacon, eggs and bread, followed up by a large mug of tea.

"There you are Tom, get that lot down you. Did you have good nights sleep?"

"Yes thanks mother, I slept like a log, didn't really want to get up this morning."

"We'll be sailing in a while mother, can you pack a bottle for Tom and I please?" asked Jimmy.

Mother gave both Jimmy and I a bottle of rum to take on the trip with us, apparently tradition with the house. Dressed fed and ready, we said our farewells to mother and headed for the harbour and Jimmy's boat.

"See you in a couple of day's mother." Jimmy shouted as he turned and waved his farewells.

"Well Tom! Are you looking forward to sailing today? It will be good to get the smell of fish on you again, wont it?"

"Aye Jimmy, I can't wait to see how you Lowestoft chaps fish, its going to be a different experience to me."

A few minutes walk saw us entering the harbour, there was a bustle of vessels coming and going, some heavy in the water with fish, others running out to sea; their holds empty on the hopes of a good catch. The breeze was light with a bright sun beaming down on the dark tanned sails, a wonderful picture for the sorest eyes.

"Busy place this." I commented to Jimmy. ."I've never seen so many fishing boats gathered in one place."

"That it is Tom, there's not far short of three hundred vessels working out of here, that's without the visiting boats that call in to unload their catches. It gets pretty crowded at times."

I watched for a while in amazement at the variety of fishing boats that were in the harbour, ranging from fourteen to sixty feet plus in length. Some had trawl nets whilst others were carrying pots and longlines, crabbers, whelk boats cod liners, a vast variety of boats of all descriptions.

"Here we are Tom! .... Morning all!" shouted Jimmy as he leaned over the rail on the harbour wall, looking down onto the Jane-Ellen below.

The vessel was some sixty feet in length, brightly varnished and very well kept, a fine ship, and one that the roughest skipper would be proud of.

I followed Jimmy down the ladder and jumped aboard the boat, the crew of two were busy sorting out the two large beam trawls that were lying on each side of the deck, preparing them for the forthcoming trip. I had worked beam trawls before but these two were almost as long as the boat it's self,

"Good morning Jimmy." the crew bade as we found our feet on the deck.

Jimmy replied politely to the two lads, which continued to beaver away at the tasks they had in hand.

"We've got a new hand lads. I would like you to meet Tom, he's a Deal chap, one of the best fishermen on that part of the coast."

I was greeted by the men, who with rapid and fast words welcomed me aboard, asking many questions as to my experience and seamanship skills, never stopping for a minute as it seemed they hadn't time to ease off on their chores.

"Hang on lads, just stop work for a minute, that's it, come over here." Jimmy said as he leant against the rail.

The two men stopped what they were doing and came over to where Jimmy and I were standing.

"Yes Jimmy, what's the trouble, we done something wrong have we?" They asked almost simultaneously.

"This is Tom as I've just said; now he's going to be sailing with us and be a part of the crew on this boat. I would like you to stop what you are doing for a while and show him the ropes; he's only been used to small beach boats you see. But first Tom would like to introduce himself properly and tell you a bit about himself and how he came to meet me, then we will all know each other, wont we? There's plenty of time before we sail, so don't rush, beside I have got to get the charts sorted out before casting off, right, you carry on and put the crew put in the picture Tom, I'll see you all see you in a minute."

Jimmy went below, leaving me with his two deck hands, who by now had made themselves comfortable and were sitting on the hatch cover, waiting for my story.

"Well lads, this is how it is, or was as the case may be. My name's Tom, as you know already know, and I hail from Deal in Kent." I went on to tell the two lads of my encounter with Jimmy and how I came to be stranded, eventually landing in Lowestoft.

"Well that's about the top and tail of it lads, now you know all about me."

Exchanging a few details between each other, the two lads then got up and continued with the work they had previously been engaged in. Jimmy had now just returned aloft and had sat down next to me, just managing to listen to the last of what I had to say.

"A bit quiet aren't they Jimmy? They don't seem to have very much to say."

"Don't worry Tom, they'll talk among themselves for an hour or so, sort you out, then once we start fishing they'll take you in like you were one of their brothers. They are a bit unsure of strangers you know, it will be alright."

"If you say so Jimmy, I don't want to get in the way and upset anyone."

"Nonsense Tom! Come on; let's get the old girl to sea, looks like the lads are almost done."

He went aft and took the tiller, the wind was off the land, and the Jane-Ellen's head was facing seaward, not leaving much effort to get her underway.

"Hoist sail lads!" came the order, as the two lads prepared to hoist the large mainsail. ."Come on now; get the fore and mizzen set. Tom! Let go fore and aft, quick now."

I rushed forward and let go the fore line, the boats head shook and started to fall away from the wall, quickly I rushed aft and let go the stern line, within an instant the Jane-Ellen started to pull clear of the quay.

"Tie off lads, that's the way, here she goes, the winds got her now."

Just as the lads had finished securing the mizzen the Jane-Ellen healed slightly to starboard, taking the fresh puff of wind that bellowed out the sails, steadily she gathered way and started to move gracefully towards the harbour entrance. We hadn't very far to go to reach the entrance to the harbour, just a matter of a couple of minutes, then once clear of the wall it would be all plain sailing and out to the fishing grounds.

"Come aft Tom. You lads can lay too now, nothing to worry about today, the seas too calm for any trouble."

Making my way aft, I joined Jimmy at the tiller, watching as the Jane-Ellen gracefully pushed her way through the water, cutting a foaming creamy white crest each side of her bows, as she pushed her way onward to the east and into the glow of the red morning sky.

"Aye Jimmy, what will you be wanting?" I asked as I sat down beside him.

"You know these waters don't you Tom? You've sailed them before on a few occasions haven't you?"

"Aye somewhat Jimmy, I've been up this way a few times piloting, but I'm not sure of the fishing grounds though."

"Well take the helm; it will give you a chance to get the feel of the old girl before we start fishing, our course is north east true. Here you are Tom, grab a hold."

I took the tiller of the Jane-Ellen, and moved it slowly from side to side to get the feel of her under way; she responded to the slightest movement and handled perfectly.

"Well Tom, how do you like her, runs well under a good set of canvas, doesn't she?"

"She handles very well Jimmy, a good response from the slightest movement on the tiller."

"Well I'm off for a few hours sleep now Tom, won't get much once fishing starts, one of the lads will stay on deck with you in case you need any help. Give me a shout at mid-day."

"No problem Jimmy, I'll shout you at mid-day." I replied as Jimmy's head disappeared below.

The lad that was left on deck with me sat up forward, staring me in the eyes, not saying a word. I remembered what Jimmy had said and took no notice of him. Finding my course I settled back and let the Jane-Ellen run before the wind, watching the other fishing boats slowly fall astern of us. She certainly had a good rate of knots in a light breeze; heaven knows what she would do in a stiff blow.

My thoughts turned to home and old Harry, wondering what he was up to, and when I might get back. The lad up forward suddenly rose to his feet and came aft, then sat down beside me, looking quietly at my pose, then spoke.

"I'm John; you certainly know your stuff in handling a boat Tom. Don't you?"

"Aye John, I've been doing it for a few years now, not much in calm weather like this though, usually leave those kind of days for the boys." I answered, cunningly.

"Aye Tom, I think we are going to get on just fine, aye that I do."

"I hope so John, I certainly hope so, but I might need a bit of help with certain things as I've never been fishing on a large vessel like the Jane-Ellen before." I said gaining a bit more of his confidence.

We settled back together, talking and exchanging views on fish and fishing, whiling away the hours as if they were minutes.

."Well its almost noon John, will you go and give Jimmy a shake please?"

"Aye Tom, right away."

John went below and called Jimmy and the other lad up on deck, without any orders being given, the two lads slackened off the sheets then started preparing the trawl for shooting, certainly a well trained crew, I thought to myself.

Jimmy made his way aft and took the helm from me, easing the Jane-Ellen back into the wind in order to ease off her way, or slow the ship down for those that are unfamiliar with sea jargon.

"Any problems Tom?" Jimmy asked as I shook my head to his answer.

"Right lets get the gear over the side lads, Tom you man the winch," he said as I made my way to the winch and took up my position." Let it go." Came the orders from Jimmy.

The two lads lowered the large beam trawl over the side of the Jane-Ellen and down into the sea, the cod end was then thrown overboard and the beam trawl pulled away from the side of the boat, slowly falling astern as we made way beam onto the wind. Steadily the winch brake was released and the warp was paid out allowing the trawl to descend to the seabed, it didn't take long for the trawl to disappear beneath the crystal clear blue sea. I kept the brake slightly on to stop the net overturning as it descended to the seabed, the winch groaned and vibrated under the pressure now being put upon it as fathom after fathom of warp was released from the winch drum as the trawl sunk deeper and deeper down to the bottom.

"Stop her at eighty fathoms Tom." Shouted Jimmy across the noise of the grumbling winch.

"Will do Jimmy ten fathoms to go; nine; eight; seven. That's it Jimmy, eighty fathoms of warp out, the brakes are on and all is fast and secure." I informed him as I locked off the winch to stop any more warp running free.

The Jane-Ellen came up with a sudden jerk as the full weight of the trawl, now on the seabed, was taken; slowly she started to pull the trawl along the sea bed, all sails straining to their uttermost as the heavy weight below pulled at the boat. The two lads secured the towing warp in a block which was situated on the stern, making it easier for the Jane-Ellen to be steered.

"That's her Jimmy." Shouted John as he finished securing the warp in the block.

We were now trawling, although similar to what we did back home, there actually was no comparison, everything was bigger and heavier, a Deal boat would never be able to pull this gear, if it did, it would be impossible to haul it back again without the help of a winch. At Deal we fished in shallow water, not venturing out much further than a few miles. Here, we were some sixty miles out to sea, pulling gear bigger and heavier than I thought it was possible to pull, but here it was, on the seabed and being pulled along, although a strain on the boat.

The crew started getting boxes up from within the Jane-Ellen's hold, stowing them up on the fore deck ready to be filled up with fish, that's hopefully if we caught any, moving aft, I rejoined Jimmy at the tiller and sat beside him.

"What do you recon Tom? Tows well in a mild breeze, doesn't she?"

"Aye Jimmy she sure does, there's certainly some weight there to pull. Tell me, how long do you tow for?"

"Well the bottoms smooth and sandy here, we generally tow for about two hours, a bit longer today as its calmer, that way we will cover a greater area of ground, here take the tiller for a while Tom."

Jimmy moved from his position and left me to take control of the tiller, she was effortless to handle even with the tremendous weight dragging behind her, and was making a good three knots as well.

"What course are you set on Jimmy?" I asked leaning over the long wooden tiller arm to attract his attention.

"Oh! It doesn't really matter today Tom, its calm enough. I tell you what; you take her where you think you might find some fish, get a good haul and show the lads how a Deal man's luck is, ok."

He sniggered slightly then took out a pouch of tobacco and a pipe from his jacket pocket, filled the pipe and started puffing great clouds of smoke into the air, the breeze carrying the smoke across the bows and off across the sea, where it dispersed into thin air.

Thoughtfully I stared at the sun which had now become almost stationed directly above us; the wind was still very light and from the sou'west. Right I thought to myself as I pushed the tiller over to starboard, I had decided in my mind that towing due east might be a good idea, why I don't know, but something told me that east was the direction to tow in. Strange how one gets a feeling to do the opposite to what everyone else would do, isn't it, over she went onto the port tack, the crew automatically adjusting her trim, Jimmy looked at me with surprise obviously wondering why I had decided to alter course, but he never said a word..

"You did say that you left it to me where I wanted to tow Jimmy." I commented as his eyes met mine. ."I just felt that east was lucky, that's all."

"You carry on Tom, go where you want, there's nothing to hurt around this area, the bottoms smooth and clear."

Jimmy settled back onto the deck and was soon joined by the two crew hands, enjoying a spot of sunshine while they had the chance. Their eyes kept turning towards me, then glancing at the direction in which I was steering the Jane-Ellen, and then they whispered quietly to one and other.

I could tell that somewhere along the line the subject of their discussion was obviously me and something to do with the heading I was on, well I knew nothing of trawling in the North Sea, I'd never trawled this area before, and so it was all trial and error. Almost one and a half hours had passed without a word being spoken to me, which enlightened my concern. Right I though, we'll have her up, meaning I had decided that it was time to haul the trawl.

"Time to haul Jimmy, I think we've got enough fish in her now."

Jimmy turned and looked at me with surprise, the two crew members starting to laugh heavily behind his back.

"What's up Jimmy done something wrong have I? Or have I missed the joke." I asked a bit uneasily.

"It's only been an hour and half Tom, a bit too early to haul yet, beside there won't be enough fish in her."

"Why not Jimmy, what makes you so sure there's no fish in the gear yet, tell me what's the joke?"

"Oh not much Tom, we decided to have a laugh with you, this being your first trip and all that, so we dropped the trawl on a patch of barren ground, there's never any fish here, at least we've never had a good haul in this area."

They all started laughing loudly again, making me feel quite low and somewhat stupid, what the hell, I thought; they're not having one over on me like this., I'll show them.

."I suppose you think I don't know what I'm doing then? Well, we will have the net up anyway, she's pretty full now and I think its time to haul."

"Have it your own way Tom, you stay there and we'll get the net in for you, sorry you couldn't take a joke."

Laughingly they unblocked the trawl warp from the stern, slackened the sheets on the mainsail and powered up the steam driven winch. The gear was engaged and hissing and grinding the winch slowly started to wind in the trawl warp. Every fathom hauled seemed to make the winch groan harder, until with a great strain it almost stopped hauling in the warp, the Jane Ellen meanwhile had taken on a good list as she beckoned to the weight of gear hanging from her beam some fathoms below.

"What's the problem Jimmy, is the winch playing up a bit, or have you forgotten what to do?" I remarked sarcastically, hoping to get my own back on them.

"It seems like we might have picked something up in the net Tom, its getting damned heavy now, there's a bit too much strain on the old winch."

The trawl was now directly below our keel, some ten fathoms down, and the Jane-Ellen was listing a bit further over to port as the full weight of the net and whatever was in it took charge.

"Full of bloody rocks and rubbish I expect!" Jimmy exclaimed.

Slowly the winch, grunting and grinding, strained heavily to pull the trawl up to the surface and alongside the boat, inch by inch it steadily rose upwards.

"Nearly there Jimmy." Shouted John as he peered over the side to see how far the trawl had to come up. ."That's it! Hold it there."

Jimmy stopped the winch, secured the brakes to stop the trawl from falling back onto the seabed, then leaning over the side, stared down into the net to see what was causing all the weight.

"Something very heavy in her lads, I can't quite make out what it is. Drop the sails and we will get in inboard."

The lads dropped the sails as ordered, and then fetched two large rope beckets; these were placed around the forward shoe of the beam trawl then secured to a double purchase lifting block.

"Haul away John, steady now, steady as you got! Hold it there."

Jimmy tied off the fore beam as it fell inboard, then the whole procedure was repeated on the aft beam shoe.

"Is she all secure lads? Good! Tom, get that block hitched onto the back strop, smart now."

I hooked the block into the back strop; this was used to haul the cod end aboard.

"Haul away steady John, slowly now." Ordered Jimmy as John took a turn around the capstan head and started hauling.

Slowly and steadily the trawl came up out of the water and started to fall inboard over the rail.

"I don't believe it." Said Jimmy with a look of surprise on his face.

As the cod end came out of the water, it took Jimmy by surprise, hauling it up and swinging part of it over the rail, it hung there bulging out almost as wide as the boats beam, glistening with brown and white streaks, there was still another thirty plus feet of the cod end hanging over the side yet, and just as full.

"I still don't believe it!" Jimmy stuttered, with a look of shock in his eyes. ."We have never caught anything on this patch of ground before, come on lads lets get it aboard."

The cod end had to be lifted aboard in three separate lifts owing to the weight of fish it contained, untying the cod end the fish were released and rushed out onto the deck, plaice, hundreds of good quality plaice, covering the deck from port to starboard almost two feet deep.

"That was a stroke of luck Tom, just a stroke of beginners luck."

"Not really Jimmy." I answered."It's us Deal chaps you know, we just get these feelings, and….well some how they always seem to pay off."

Sniggering at the three of them, I commenced helping with clearing the trawl so that it could be shot again for another tow.

"You've done alright on that tow Tom, not such a bad skipper after all eh?" was the first decent remark I got from John.

"Yes we know John, its luck that's all, just pure luck." Jimmy replied

"Why! Do I detect a bit of jealousy in that remark Jimmy?" I laughingly commented.

"No Tom, but if you think it was skill, well then let's see you do the same again, come on lads; get the trawl over the side, Tom's going to fill it up again for us." He said as they all once more started laughing.

The trawl was quickly lowered overboard, sails were set again and I took the helm, I only hoped there were fish here and it wasn't just luck. It wasn't going to be so easy this time as we had to tack up and down against the wind to get a similar sort of tow near to the last one, we now had to beat to windward and hope she could still pull the gear ok.

"All secure Tom, you just stay on the tiller mate, I'll help the lads gut the fish and box up."

Once more I settled back into steering the Jane-Ellen, whilst Jimmy and the lads washed and boxed up the fish, then cleaned and scrubbed the deck down ready for the next haul.

"Well Jimmy, what do you recon we made in stoneage on that tow mate?"

"Looking at the boxes Tom, I would say we passed the two hundred stone mark easily, good prime fish as well."

The next hour saw the decks get slowly cleared, with the fish all being boxed and stowed below, everything was washed clean and the decks shone again as if nothing had ever touched them. I decided to haul early, just in case the first haul was a fluke, and there were no more fish on this so called barren ground, didn't want to waste time towing around here for nothing.

"Ready to haul Jimmy, are you fit lads, come on lets get the gear up."

"What already Tom! She hasn't had a long enough tow yet surely, it's shorter than the last one."

"I think she has Jimmy, I think she has, and there should be enough in her by now." I said hopefully.

"Come on lads, Tom thinks he knows what he's doing. Let's get her up."

Once again the main sheet was slackened, the winch engaged, and the trawl was heaved slowly towards the Jane-Ellen. Creaking and grinding under the strain the winch slowly struggled to heave the heavy net to the surface.

"Hold it there John, put the bakes on mate." I shouted as the trawl came crashing against the side.

The beam was secured alongside and Jimmy's face once again lit up, then turned red, and a bit embarrassed he said to me.

"You've done it again Tom, I don't believe it, I thought it was impossible, but you've done it again!"

Sure enough as the nets came aboard and the cod end was released, hundreds of plaice scattered themselves all over the deck.

"Looks as much again as the first haul lads." Jimmy shouted excitedly.

"Come on; let's get her clear and back overboard again, two more catches like this and we'll be going ashore early, and full to the gunwales."

The trawl was once again lowered to the seabed and fishing begun.

"You stay at the tiller Tom, you're doing alright. I'll help clear the decks."

Settling back once more for another tow, I watched as Jimmy and the crew sorted the fish out and cleared the decks. Dark had now begun to fall upon us and time for another haul. Again this proved to be almost as good a haul as the previous two, with plenty of fish coming aboard. Two more good hauls were had, and by daylight of the following morning we had enough fish on board to make a good trip, with the Jane-Ellen sitting low in the water from the weight of her cargo it was decided to stop fishing and make for home.

"That's enough lads." Jimmy said. "Come on lets go home, here Tom, you help finish off with the crew, I'll take the helm now."

Passing the helm to Jimmy I went amidships and helped the two crew lads to clear the decks. The hold was full to the top with prime plaice leaving some boxes to be stowed on the deck. The wind had now freshened slightly and swung round to the nor'east, this would make it an easy passage back to port, as we would have a following sea and wind, an easy run home.

"It looks like we're in for a blow from the nor'east lads." Jimmy shouted from the stern.

"Aye it does look a bit threatening doesn't it Jimmy?" I replied as I joined him at the helm.

"What do you reckon Jimmy, did well didn't we? The catch should make quite a good penny shouldn't it? All prime fish as well."

"Aye that you did Tom, we've a good catch the best we've had for some weeks now, mother will be pleased. You get below now and grab a couple of hours sleep, you've earned it mate, I'll shout you when we sight land."

"Thanks Jimmy, I could use a couple of hours rest. I'll see you later."

I went below, lay on the bunk and before I had time to close my eyes, had fallen asleep, the first in twenty four hours.

During my period below, and quite unbeknown to me as I was deep in the world of sleep, the wind had stiffened up freshly from the north east. Some three hours had passed when a shout came rumbling across my dreams.

"Tom! Tom! Come on mate you're wanted on deck."

Sleepily my eyes opened to find John standing over me, dressed in his oilskins and dripping wet from top to toe.

"Come on Tom; wake up, Jimmy wants you on deck at once, hurry up now."

."What's up John?" I asked rubbing my eyes as I sat up on my bunk, staring at his dripping wet clothes.

"You've to come on deck Tom, the winds freshened fast, there's a lot of sea running now, come on hurry up."

."Ok John I'll be with you in a minute, let me get my boots and oilskins on."

John went back topside leaving me to sort myself out; the Jane-Ellen was rolling heavily, throwing me from side to side across my bunk. Quickly dressing and coming to my full senses I climbed the companion ladder and came upon the deck, the wind was blowing a good gale from the north east, and the seas were being lifted high above us with their tops breaking into large curling foaming fists, each one throwing tons of water upon the already heavy laden Jane-Ellen as they broke over her side. Looking quickly around I saw that we were running under reefed sail but still going through the water with lightening speed, Jimmy was waving his arms and beckoning me towards him.

"Tom." he shouted above the roar of the wind." Tom come aft quick!"

Rushing aft I grabbed the tiller alongside Jimmy, almost being thrown over board by a large sea which decided to crash down on the Jane-Ellen's deck.

"Where'd this lot come from Jimmy?" I asked as I finally found my footing.

"It just came up like a bat out of hell Tom, lot more to come as well looking at the sea that's running now, here grab a hold of the helm for a minute, I'm going to give the lads a hand to put the storm mainsail up, there's too much wind to carry her on the sail she's running on, It'll split her wide open."

Grabbing hold of the rail, Jimmy left and went forward, where the two lads were struggling to pull the large mainsail out of the fore locker. The full weight of the Jane-Ellen suddenly came to my arms, she was running on a beam wind making some nine knots; being heavily laden with her cargo of fish, she was harder than normal to steer, every beam sea tried to throw her head around threatening to capsize her. Strenuously I struggled to gain control of my situation, and with great effort managed to master the helm.

Jimmy and the crew meanwhile had lowered the main sail, just leaving the jib and mizzen sails up to keep the Jane-Ellen under way, as they were trying to bend on the storm sail, the seas were running clean over her decks covering the trio and constantly threatening to heave them overboard. Steering became harder with just a jib and mizzen flying; how she didn't capsize I don't know.

At last the mainsail was once again hoisted and full way gained on the Jane-Ellen, this storm sail was a quarter the size of the usual main sail and made of much thicker and stronger canvas, it was especially designed for rough conditions.

"That's that done." Gasped Jimmy as he came crashing back along side me, almost being dragged off his feet by the huge sea that caught him as it run a foot deep across the deck.

"Everything ok Jimmy?" I asked as I spat out a mouthful of seawater.

"Aye it's alright now Tom, bloody weather, its good job we packed up fishing when we did, I wouldn't want to be fishing in this sea, or trying to dodge it, Its not very pleasant."

He settled on the tiller arm with me, looking into the mouth of the storm at the dark black clouds that were running in from the east, shaking his head in disaprovement of the weather conditions that had now come upon us.

"We've about thirty miles to go before we reach port Tom, it should take us about four hours in this weather, and hopefully the tide will be up then. Bad job out here now, isn't it?"

"Aye that it is, it certainly came out of nowhere fast." I answered.

I knew the waters in this region and what could happen off the harbour entrance with a storm force easterly blowing, it was no pretty situation.

"Are you alright on the helm for a while Tom? I'm going below to put some dry clothes on."

"Aye Jimmy you carry on. You can count on me; if I need a hand in a hurry I'll give you a shout."

Jimmy knew he could trust me to bring the Jane-Ellen safely back to port, this wasn't the first time I had been caught in this area in a full gale; I knew the area pretty well.

It was nearly three hours before Jimmy and the crew showed their faces above deck again, all this time I had been fighting against the seas in order to keep the Jane-Ellen afloat and running home.

"How's it going Tom?" asked Jimmy as he looked at our position.

"Almost at the harbour entrance Jimmy, not far to go now, I can just make out the lights on the shore in the distance."

"Here Tom I'll take her now, it's going to be tricky getting through the entrance with the old girl in this sea, she's so heavy in the water she won't respond to commands quickly, give her here mate."

I passed the tiller over to Jimmy, leaving him in control; after all it was his boat. Clinging on to the mizzen mast to stop myself being washed overboard, I watched as we approached the harbour entrance.

Huge seas were being tossed high up above the harbour walls, momentarily hiding the view of the shore behind them. A heavy backwash was raging in the mouth of the harbour, throwing huge amounts of water in unpredictable directions. Jimmy glanced at me looking somewhat disturbed.

"What do you reckon on our chance Jimmy?" I asked as another sea came aboard and filled my mouth.

"In normal conditions and without the weight in her hold, I wouldn't shake an eye Tom, but she's heavy in the water, and with this following sea she doesn't want to answer to the helm so good."

He stared again at the towers of water being thrown high over the harbour wall, pausing for a moment in deep thought before finally making a decision on what to do.

"We're going in." he shouted.

"You two lads get ready to drop the main sail as soon as we get in the entrance, the jib'll take her through, Tom, slacken the main sheets, we're going in!"

As I slackened the mainsheets letting the sail blow over her beam, Jimmy turned the Jane-Ellen's head towards the harbour entrance, the might of the wind and sea was directly astern of us, blowing us even faster towards the harbour. Her bows dipped down on every swell as they ran underneath her, forcing tons of water up and over the deck and at times almost submerging the old girl, running from fore to aft almost a foot deep until it was released out of the scuppers, ridding her of the extra unwelcome burden.

"Get ready lads here we go!" shouted Jimmy and he grasped the tiller hard in both hands.

Rushing at a great speed of knots the Jane-Ellen entered the towering broken water in the harbour entrance, disappearing beneath the tons of water that was thrown upon her deck.

"Down sail, let go the mizzen sheet Tom, quickly now you lot, there's no time to waste."

The main dropped to the deck rapidly, the lads were hanging onto the main mast in the hopes of not being washed overboard as I slackened off the mizzen sheet; Jimmy was struggling to hold the Jane-Ellen's head before the wind, while the Jane-Ellen continued at great speed through the harbour entrance.

"Grab a hold here Tom, I can't hold her on my own, hold on tight!" shouted Jimmy to me as I made a leap towards him and took a hold on the tiller arm.

A large sea suddenly broke over our stern, covering the decks with some twelve inches of water, the bows went under and started to sheer towards the harbour wall, and the whole boat shook and shivered as she tried to rid herself of the extra burden.

"Pull Tom pull!"

Struggling for dear life we managed in a split second to bring the boat's head back round, she lifted high on the next sea shaking herself clear of water, as if she were proudly showing off to the spectators that lined the shore, who were watching our attempt to enter the harbour.

"Look out Tom!"

Before Jimmy finished his sentence another huge sea broke over her stern, filling her from stem to stern with water again, she hesitated momentarily, as if some giant hand was trying to drag her to the bottom, then again lifted high on the following sea shaking her decks clear of the tons of water that were lying on them.. A final burst of speed saw us through the entrance and into safe calmer water inside the shelter of the harbour.

"Tighten in on the mizzen sheet, slacken the jib." Ordered Jimmy as he released his grip on the tiller and thanked me for my assistance.

Orders were quickly followed, the head of the Jane-Ellen came round into the wind, and she lay wallowing motionless, pleased to be in the safety of the harbour walls. A small punt came alongside; this had been lying just inside the entrance waiting to aid us in case things went wrong, they weren't needed though thank God.

."That was a narrow thing Jimmy." One of the men in the punt shouted.

"Are you ok there? You're lying heavy in the water, sprung a leak have you? We didn't expect to see you back for another two days or more mates."

By now Jimmy and the rest of us had gathered ourselves together, somewhat wet but safe and started to furl the sails up ready for docking.

"No mates." he answered laughing. ."We haven't sprung any planks, just had a fortunate trip, we're full of prime fish, here grab a hold of this line and take it ashore will you."

"Full of fish." The man answered as he grabbed hold of the line that had been thrown to him. ."You haven't been out long enough to catch a cold."

They started rowing the small punt towards the wall taking our line with them.

"Drop the other sails lads we're safe now, lets get her alongside."

The rope had been secured ashore and we pulled the Jane-Ellen into the wall, stern lines and springs were secured and the Jane-Ellen was finally motionless, we were in.

"Well mates we've done a good job, if I say so myself, you two lads get the hatches off, Tom and I will go ashore and organize a party to get her unloaded, we won't be long."

We stepped ashore leaving the lads to sort the boat out. Dozens of men were gathering around waiting for the chance of some work unloading our catch, and the buyer had also arrived, making his way to Jimmy.

"Good catch Jimmy what have you got on board today, any prime?"

"Mostly prime plaice mate; about a thousand stone or so I should recon without counting it."

The buyer, along with the crowd that overheard the news, was taken aback by Jimmy's catch, and unbelievingly questioned Jimmy's answer.

"As much as that Jimmy! In two days? That's just almost impossible; it's never been done before by any boat here."

"Aye, and on the barren ground as well, Tom here was the skipper for the trip though, not I." Jimmy answered as he pointed to me and smiled.

"Right I want eight of the best men. Who's here now? You,… you…. And you." Jimmy picked out eight sturdy men for unloading.

"How are you getting on lads, everything onboard all secure and ready yet?"

"Yes all ready Jimmy, the sails are furled and the hatches are open ready to unload her."

"Right you eight men get to work and mind you wash her clean when you've finished unloading, or there'll be no pay for you later, come on lads leave them to it."

The two crew hands joined us ashore leaving the eight men to unload and clear down the Jane-Ellen.

"The days yours now lads, Tom and I will see you here at eight in the morning I'll let you know the good news then, off you go now."

The lads went their way and we went ours, home to Jimmy's house and to let mother know the good news about the great catch we had.

The short distance to Jimmy's house took but a few minutes, mother was standing anxiously at the gate, with tears glistening in her eyes.

"Hello mother." Jimmy said.

She rushed towards him and threw her arms around him, trying to hold back her tears.

"Jimmy, oh Jimmy I was so worried."

"Worried mother, by what?"

"I watched as you approached the harbour, and….well, the Jane-Ellen looked like she was sinking, she was nearly under the water, how you got in I don't know Jimmy, the seas are tremendous, and thank God you're safe. And Tom are you alright lad? Oh it's good to see you."

."Its alright mother, the sea is a bit on the rough side but we made it, there's not even a scratch on the old girl. Is there Tom?"

"No, not a scratch, cheer up mother, we're all safe and home now. Jimmy's got some very good news for you. Haven't you Jimmy?"

"Have you son? But what about the Jane-Ellen, what's up with her son? She looks as though she's nearly under, there must be something wrong. I did worry so."

"The Jane-Ellen's ok mother, come inside the house and Tom and I will get some dry clothes on and tell you all about our trip."

We entered the grand old house and momentarily stopped short at the smell of roast beef, which seemed to be curling its way around the picture clad walls, bringing hunger to the fullest stomach.

"That smells good mother." I commented as my sea boot went sliding across the hallway floor after I had kicked it off, leaving a trail of water droplets in its track. ."Sorry mother, it wouldn't come off, here give me a cloth and I'll clean it up."

After releasing my other sea boot with almost the same misfortune and placing it outside to dry in the wind, I proceeded to clean up the mess I had made on the floor.

"Now boys, go and get some dry clothes on and then come and sit yourselves down at the dinner table, the foods cooked and I'll serve it straight away. Off you go now."

We both went to our rooms and changed into some welcoming warm dry clothes, then returned to the dining room, and took our places at the large dining table, followed closely by mother and two heaped plates of dinner. Roast beef, roast potatoes, cabbage, carrots, we had everything. Mother put the plates on the table in front of us and then went and brought her own dinner in, placed it on the table, pulled out a chair and sat down, smiling slightly.

"Now Jimmy, tell me what's wrong with the Jane-Ellen, why are you back from your trip so early? No lies now."

Jimmy and I went on during dinner to tell mother what had befallen on the trip, how I had been teased on the barren ground, and how by luck we had loaded the Jane-Ellen full of prime plaice, mother smiled contentedly at the news of our fruitful trip.

"So you see mother, that's the whole story, old Tom here did well for his first trip, didn't he?"

"Jimmy has always had good luck Tom, but never as good as that. Are you staying with us now Tom?"

A moments silence passed over the room as my reply was anxiously waited for, what could I say.

"Sorry mother, its not that you haven't made me welcome, but …. Well you see, I want to go home really, you can understand that, cant you? Besides, old Harry owes me some wages."

"Please Tom, think about staying, Jimmy and I love having you around, and you seem to get on so well together, please think about it Tom."

I looked at mother as she hid her face in her shawl, trying to hide the tears that were beginning to glisten in her eyes, poor old soul, but I couldn't stay, I didn't belong here; besides everyone back home would be worried as to where I had gone, no one knew where I was or what had happened to me. Jimmy sat staring at me from the other side of the table; quiet and almost motionless. I could almost read what was going through his mind

"Tell you what!" I said." I'll think the situation over again tonight, and give you a definite answer in the morning, no promises though of me staying."

Mother jumped up with joy, planting a big kiss on my right cheek.

"Thanks Tom! You mind that you give plenty of thought to staying, mother and I would love to have you stay with us." Said Jimmy looking at me with an enlightened smile.

"Yes I certainly will Jimmy, but should I decide to stay, just should mind you, I will still have to go home to Deal at some time and sort my business out. My family will be wondering where I have got to, I haven't seen them since I left Deal that day to go mackerel fishing in the Mary-Anne."

For the next couple of hours we sat around the table telling yarns and recalling pleasant incidents which had happened to us in days gone past. Outside the house, the wind had now fallen away to a fine breeze, with the sun poking its head out from behind the broken clouds.

"Looks like being a fine day again tomorrow Jimmy, we will be able to get to sea, wont we?"

"Aye Tom it looks like its fining away nicely, we will sail on the afternoon tide all going well."

"No, I didn't exactly mean with me Jimmy, just the way I said it in a manner of speaking."

"That's alright Tom, I understand, just kidding you, come on now, let's go and see how the beer is; but only one mind you."

"Aye Jimmy that's a grand idea, I'll come along with you, but mind it is only one, no more now."

We dressed in our outdoor clothes and bid mother farewell for the time being, and then made our way slowly down the little track towards the ale house. As usual the place was full to the seams with boisterous laughing and singing coming from within, almost breaking the rafters.

"In you go Tom?" Jimmy said as he opened the door for me, and beckoned me to enter.

As we entered the bar cheers of excitement and joy came towards us from all quarters from the occupants within.

"Where did you catch all the fish mates?" came the shouts from fishermen sitting in various parts of the inn.

Ordering a couple of pints of ale, Jimmy and I then sat down at the table in the centre of the room and began to tell the story of good fortune to all present. Unbelief of the position where we had caught the fish went through them all, but Jimmy convinced them that he pulled a prank on me, and bouncing back on him it actually paid off with the good catch we had.

"So that's how it was mates, nothing else to it, just sheer good fortune." Said Jimmy

The evening passed quickly as they always do when enjoying good company, and having a good time

"Well Tom I'm for bed, what say you, we've got a busy day ahead of us tomorrow?"

"Sure am Jimmy, I'm just about dead beat, a good nights sleep in a warm bed will go down just nice now."

"Come on then let's make tracks. Good night all see you in the morning."

We left the pub at around ten in the evening and making our way home, retired straight to our bedrooms for a good nights sleep.

The night passed quickly with the morning bringing bright sunshine and light westerly winds. Dressing and breakfast down us, we bade mother good morning and set off for the harbour and the fish market, anxious to see what the Jane-Ellen had raised, or grossed in money to put it in better words. The rough weather the day before hadn't stopped the activity going on in the harbour, the rush and bustle of boats and men continued as usual after its short break as though nothing had taken place.

On arriving at the Jane-Ellen we found the two crew lads busy as usual, preparing her for the next trip. She had been moved to the other side of the fish market, and a large stack of fish boxes had been placed on the wall along side her. The lads had arrived early to watch the catch being sold, then had come across to the Jane-Ellen to load the boxes aboard her, ready for another trip.

"Good morning lads, grand morning. Everything in order and going fine is it?"

"Good morning Jimmy, morning Tom, yes we not much more to do; she'll be ready for sea in a few hours."

"How did we get on at the market this morning lads, much about?"

"Aye Jimmy our catch." He laughed." Apart from that not much. Those landing during the night have good catches, but it's all cod, we are the only boat to land any plaice."

"That's good news anyway Tom, How much did they fetch John?"

"I think if you see the seller yourself Jimmy, it will be quite a surprise."

"Thanks John, you two alright here are you? Tom and I will go and find out what we grossed on the last trip."

"Aye Jimmy you two go. Bill and I will get the old girl ready for sea, see you later."

Jimmy and I left the lads to finish loading the boat and get her ready for the next trip; we then headed for the fish market to see how much the catch had made.

"Two of the best those lads Tom. I would be hard pressed to find another couple like them."

"Jimmy." I said quietly." About staying on, well! Well; it's not that I don't like the work or anything, but!"

"That's alright Tom, you think about it, no hurry now we've got all day."

"No Jimmy I have given it a lot of thought. I would like to stay on but...."

"But what Tom, you know mother would be glad to have you stay with us if you want to."

"No it's not that, it's just....well no one at home knows where I am, they must be worrying. Beside I have my pay to get from old Harry, quite a pretty penny, so you see I must go home."

"Tom if you must go then I won't stop you, but if you want to come back there's a job here for you. When do you intend to go?"

"As soon as I can find a berth going that way I guess, I'm going to have a wander around the harbour in a while and see if anyone is going south."

"Look leave it for the minute Tom; let's see how much we made, I'll have a chat with a couple of mates of mine shortly, see if I can fix you up with any of the things you need. Come on there's our salesman."

"Charlie." he shouted as we moved across to a large tall rugged man dressed in a white coat.

"Good morning Jimmy, how you going, did alright for yourselves on that last trip. Didn't you?"

"Not bad Charlie I guess considering the weather conditions, this is Tom my skipper of the last trip."

I was introduced to Charlie and given the eye over, followed by an approving smile.

"You're not from these parts are you lad, by the sound of your tongue?" was the comment.

"No Charlie I come from Deal, just a visit you know, I had to show old Jimmy how to catch fish." I answered laughing.

"Good chap is Jimmy, one of the best. So you're the one who caught those plaice are you? Splendid catch, good run of fish too, made a pretty penny as well; you caught the market just right with that storm blowing, there's been no other plaice landed, only cod. Come with me to the office and I'll tell you how much you grossed."

We followed Charlie to his small office at the other end of the market. A small square box shaped shed, looking more in resemblance to a pile of old broken fish boxes joined together than a fish seller's office.

"Come in mates, come on in. Now where did I put that book?" he said mumbling to himself.

Turning over a pile of old paper and books, Charlie, still muttering to himself rummaged about looking for what was his day book.

"Well bugger me, old age and worry must be taking its toll on me, it's in my pocket."

Taking the book out of his coat pocket, he opened it and ran his fingers over the pages.

"Here we are Jimmy, the Jane-Ellen. I sold the lot, went fast too."

Mumbling away under his breath he began to write some figures down on an old scrap piece of paper.

"That's it; here you are Jimmy, one thousand six hundred and twenty seven stone. All plaice, apart from eleven stone, and of course a cod that I took out for my dear old wife. Didn't mind did you?"

"It would have been all the same if we did wouldn't it Charlie?" replied Jimmy shaking his head.

"Ah I knew you wouldn't mind, especially as old Charlie here fetched you a good price for your catch, a lot more than it usually makes. Wait a minute let me tell you what it fetched."

Scribbling again on an old piece of paper he began to add up the total value of our catch, rubbing out and writing down the figures several times before completing his sums.

"There you are Jimmy got it at last; Less my commission and handling fees, you've made four hundred and twenty pounds, not a bad days work eh! Beats the port record that does."

"Thank you Charlie you can have the cod for nothing, thanks for your effort."

"I knew you would be pleased Jimmy, look I've got fish to sell, got to get back to the market now, I'll see you later."

"Ok Charlie we'll see you later."

With the results of our catch now known, Jimmy and I left the market and made our way back to the Jane-Ellen.

"You carry on Tom; I'll catch you up in a minute, just got to go and see someone, I won't be long."

Jimmy left me and made his way over to a small Barque that had come into the harbour some hours earlier, and which was lying against the wall, just up a bit from the Jane-Ellen. Back at the boat the two lads had all but completed the stowing of the fish boxes, anxious as I came aboard to see what the catch had made.

"How did we do Tom did we make a good grossing today?" asked John with a huge grin across his face.

Not knowing how the shares were divided or what percentage of the catch the crew received I declined to give an answer.

"Not bad lads, Jimmy will put you in the picture when he comes back, he won't be long. Oh by the way, I won't be sailing with you in the morning I have got to return home."

The lads were disappointed with my decision, but after explaining what I had to do, wished me good fortune and asked me to hurry back as they too didn't want to lose me.

Jimmy came back to the Jane-Ellen with a sort of upsetting smile on his face, and then sitting on the hatch called us all around.

"I suppose you've heard about Tom lads haven't you, him wanting to leave us and return home?"

"Aye Tom told us."

"It's a pity but there we go. Tom! See that Barque over there?" Jimmy said as he turned and pointed in the direction of the ship his was talking about.

"Aye Jimmy you mean the one that's berthed just ahead of the Jane-Ellen I presume."

"Yes that's the one, well her captain, nice old soul he is, well he said if you work your passage he'll take you aboard as he's sailing south, when he hauls up off Deal he'll hail a boat and put you ashore there. He's bound for Southampton, leaves on the night tide. If that's alright for you?"

"Aye it is Jimmy, just the ticket."

"Well you go over and see him, I'll tell the lads of their good fortune on the last trip."

Gathering myself up off the Jane-Ellen, I set a course for the Barque that was lying just ahead of us. A well looked after vessel, and heavily laden with cargo, she was called the Fox, a name that came to mind but I just couldn't remember where I had heard it. Not to worry my aim was to arrange a passage home to the Down's, the ship didn't really matter. I glanced over her decks, apart from half a dozen men playing cards on the foredeck no one else was to be seen, so climbing her rail I went aboard.

"Ahoy there mates, aboard the Fox there, is the captain about?"

The men stared at me in a sort of untrustworthy way, this was a natural behavior on any ship when a stranger came aboard, and something I was well used to.

"Well mates I haven't got all day. Is your captain about I'd like a word?"

"Yes mate what can I do for you?" came a voice from the aft deck behind.

"Are you the captain of the Fox?" I asked, turning to face the man behind me.

"Aye and what if I am who's asking after me, and what business have you here?"

"I am sir; led to I believe you are expecting me, I'm Tom from the Jane-Ellen."

"Tom….ah yes, Tom. That's right; Jimmy told me all about you, welcome aboard Tom."

He held out his hand and grasped mine, shaking it so fast it felt like it was going to drop off.

"I've come about a passage to the Downs as Jimmy has most likely told you."

"He has Tom, now, I haven't any wage paying jobs aboard this vessel, as I have already explained to Jimmy, and she's got a full crew. But if you are willing to work for food and passage I'll take you to the Downs and arrange for a boat to take you ashore. Is that any use to you Tom?"

"It'll suit me fine sir, I'm a good hand and know the waters well, done a lot of pilot work in these waters, and it'll suit me fine."

"Good Tom, come and meet the crew, they're a bit shy but don't mind them, a good bunch they are."   The captain took me forward to meet his crew, which after my life history having to be told in a short brief time, welcomed me aboard the Fox.

"You go and get your shore work sorted out Tom and we'll see you back aboard here at ten tonight. We sail at midnight, don't be late now."

"Thanks captain, I'll be back by ten."

Jumping ashore I went straight back to the Jane-Ellen, where I told Jimmy and the lads of my good fortune.

"I'm pleased for you Tom, but we will all miss you." Replied Jimmy." Come on, say your farewells to the lads then we'll go home for dinner, you can tell mother what's happening then."

I bade the lad's farewell then left with Jimmy for the house, wondering how to tell mother that I was leaving tonight, without upsetting her too much. She was a wonderful old lady and treated me like a son, although I hardly had the time to get to know her. Back at the house mother greeted us as usual, asking more questions than enough.

"Hang on a minute mother; let us get through the door." Jimmy said as he tried to quieten mother down a bit.

"Sorry Jimmy I was a bit carried away, rather anxious to see what the catch made, you two sit at the table and then we can talk over dinner."

We sat at the large table and within a few minutes plates of steaming hot food were placed before us. Sitting down, mother looked at us eagerly, waiting for one of us to speak.

"Mother?" I said. As I turned to her and looked her straight in the eyes.

"Tom, hang on mate, let me tell mother about the catch first, then you can have a talk with her."

"Sorry Jimmy, I didn't mean to be rude, just being a bit eager I suppose, you carry on."

"What's the matter Tom, you look like there's something bothering you. Is there something wrong?" asked mother.

"Nothing much mother, it's just that Jimmy wanted to give you the good news, I shouldn't have pushed in front, you carry on Jimmy."

I tried to cover up my words for a while, while Jimmy took the conversation, and told mother the good news, during the course of the dinner, Jimmy told mother all about the catch and how much we had made. What the lads had been paid, and how much the boat had taken for its share, but I wasn't mentioned.

"Well Tom, I expect you are wondering why I haven't told you how much your share is going to be. I, sure, I have a good reason."

"Aye Jimmy I was beginning to think you were not going to give me a share."

."Huh don't be silly Tom; you caught the fish didn't you? It's like this; Mother and I have decided, as we have had a very good catch to give you an equal share to the skipper, that's the same amount as I get, so Tom we are giving you eighty pounds. Is that ok with you?"

"Eighty pounds!" I exclaimed almost falling off my chair with shock. "Eighty pounds, well that's really good of you, thanks mother thanks Jimmy."

Now Tom I think you ought to tell mother what you have in mind, don't you?"

I looked at mother's smiling face not knowing where to start or how, I wasn't even sure I ought to leave at this particular time, as mother was so happy. How do I tell her I thought? I sat quiet for some moments then mother brought me to her attention.

"Well Tom, what is it you have to tell me son, good news I hope. Are you staying on with us now?"

Slowly I started to tell mother what I had arranged to do, explaining that I would miss her very much as she had been so kind to me, and promising to return as soon as possible. She moved towards me, put her arms around me and started to cry. Jimmy had left the room and was standing by the door, tears rolling down his face as he watched mother breaking her heart.

"Mother please don't cry." I said wiping the tears from my cheeks." I'll be back one day, I promise you that."

Holding her tight I kissed her on the cheek then helped her to sit down in the chair by the fire. Jimmy came back in and sat besides her saying nothing, just looking at me. How could I leave, I loved the old girl and thought the world of Jimmy; I must go home though I thought, I must. Getting up and pulling myself together, I looked at mother.

"Mother." I said." I have grown to love you like my own mother in the short time I have known you. I must go home please understand, but I'll be back, I promise."

She looked at me with a sorrowful expression on her face, tears running down either side of her cheeks and dropping into a well formed pool upon the floor, Jimmy had come over and put his arm around her and stood still holding tightly. She lifted her head for a while and glanced at Jimmy, the tears still running down the crevices of her face then gently falling into her lap, leaving a patch of wet showing on her dress. I moved towards her again and gave her a final hug, almost broken hearted myself at having to leave in such a manner.

"Tom, I'm sorry Tom, I was being selfish wasn't I. you must go home I know."

"Its nine thirty mother, I have to be aboard the Fox at ten. I have to leave now."

"It's alright Tom." Said Jimmy as he handed me an envelope. "Here's your money Tom, look after it mate, take care on your voyage, and when you get home send mother and I a letter. It will be well appreciated."

"Thanks Jimmy thanks for everything, and thanks mother, cheer up now."

I walked towards the door and picked up my gear, opened the door and bade them both farewell.

"Wait, wait a minute Tom,.." said mother with a slight uplift in her voice, ."We'll come down and see you off."

."Please don't, I would prefer to leave our farewells here please don't follow me, it will only make things harder."

I turned went out of the house and closed the door behind me, hesitating for a moment. Then putting my gear on my back, I set a course for the harbour and the Fox, not stopping or turning around for a last look around, just in case my heart took the better of me.

****

Chapter 10

<u>Homeward bound</u>

Boarding the Fox I was greeted by the captain, who grabbed my hand almost shaking it from the joints.

"Good to see you Tom!" he exclaimed." Wasn't sure if you would turn up."

"Good evening captain, not late am I?" I replied as I looked around the Barque, noticing that her full rig of sail was set, flapping in the evening breeze, waiting for the sheets to be hauled taught.

"No you're not late Tom, we've half an hour yet, but tell me; Jimmy says you are a good pilot and know the waters well down through the channel and off Deal. Is that so?"

"Aye captain. I've taken pilot of a few ships to and from these waters before. Why?"

"It's just that, well being a captain as well as an owner can present a few problems. You see, this here is the first cargo the Fox has had for a while and money is a bit short. We can't....."

"I know captain; you can't really afford a pilot, well I said I would work my passage for free and I will. You want a pilot, and then I will be your man."

"Thanks Tom. I really appreciate it greatly. The Fox is ready for sea at any time, so I'll leave her in your hands then."

"Captain! I'd be pleased if you would join me at the wheel, I'll show you the route out of here and down through the Gulls it might come in useful for another time."

"That I'll do Tom, go and stow your gear I'll shake up the crew."

I took my small bag of belongings below, and then returned on deck. It was a pretty still night as far as wind was concerned, although a light breeze was blowing from the west'ard, an ideal wind for sailing south.

"Everything ready topside captain." I asked glancing up at the sails and rigging as I returned topside.

"Aye Tom, we're waiting for you, she's all ready to cast off, give the order when you are ready."

"Let's get the old girl to sea then. She's your ship captain, you give the orders, let's make her sail."

Orders were given to haul in the sheets; lines fore and aft were cast off, and the head of the Fox swung away from the wall, listing gently to the breeze as the wind filled the sails. Slowly she pulled her way forward and out of the harbour into the open sea, gently pitching into the swells as they ran beneath her bows. I gave one last look towards the shore, thinking of Jimmy and mother and the new found friends I had left behind.

Daylight came with a bright fresh sun rising in the sky, a good sign of fine weather, I was relieved at the wheel by the first mate, who by what the captain had told me, was one of the best mates he had ever had.

"Go on Tom, get your head down, we know our way down channel from here."

"You sure mate; I'm running closer to the shore than most traders do, there are a lot of banks ahead of us."

"It's alright Tom we've done these waters before, you get below and get an hours sleep."

I left him on the wheel, as a couple of hours sleep would surely be welcomed, went below and don't remember much more for many hours until I was woken by a lot of shouting. As I jumped to my feet I was knocked over again almost as quickly. What the.... I stopped in thoughts for a moment, no! It can't be. Dressing quickly and gaining the deck, my suspicion was confirmed, we were aground, broadside on to the tide and the seas were beating at her hull heavily, threatening to rip her apart.

. What's happened captain?" I asked making my way aft to the wheel.

"She's struck a bank Tom, the mate don't quite know where we are."

Looking around I could make out the coastline to the west'ard, high cliffs to the north and low land to the south, my suspicions were confirmed by the rotating light on the high cliffs to the nor'west of us.

"Well captain, I told the mate we were running in close, but how he got right out here I don't know."

A loud bang came from within the hull, going off like a canon, and vibrating through the whole length of the ship, that was it she's breaking up.

"Captain you're stuck on the north Goodwin bar, on the outside edge of the Goodwin Sands., tides falling and it looks like she's breaking up. Why the heck didn't someone give me a shout, knowing that you've passed over shoaling water? It's a miracle you've come this far without running aground."

"It's the mate Tom, he took charge from me four hours ago, I did tell him to shout you if he needed you, but he said he was sure of where he was going Tom. What shall we do, any ideas?"

"Let the anchors go captain, that'll hold her from going on too far, but I'm afraid there's not much hope, not much comes off these banks in one piece, there's always too much tide running across here, rips the bottom out of any vessel that gets stranded."

The two large anchors were dropped over the side, clearing the hull as the Fox drove further onto the sand banks, cracking and groaning with every movement. The main mast came crashing to the deck, bringing every bit of canvas down with it, I had been asleep for some twelve hours, and with a following tide behind the ship, we had made the coast off Deal rather faster than expected. This was going to be embarrassing for me, a Deal lad rescued from the Goodwin Sands.

"Got any flares captain?" I asked

"No Tom nothing."

"Get a barrel of oil up here and secure it amidships captain, we'll set a fire going to attract attention."

A barrel of whale oil used in the lamps was brought up on deck, secured to the stump where the main mast had once been and set alight. It glowed brightly in the evening sky, lighting up the sea from some distance around us. Within a few minutes a couple of loud explosions roared out to the north of us. The North Goodwin lightship had seen our plight and was signaling the shore with cannon fire. Ten minutes passed and in the dark evening, we could make out the distant glare of a white flare coming from the beach at Deal, we had been spotted help was hopefully on the way.

"It's alright captain, there's help coming from the beach at Deal, it should be here in a couple of hours with this wind."

The captain acknowledged my findings, and another loud bang came from within the hold of the Fox, and then closely followed by another. She was being screwed into the sand by the swirling action of the tide, the sea just three feet deep around her hull now, twisted and sucked her deeper into the sand.

"One of you get below, and take a look at what's happening." Shouted the captain, who was now understandably worried about the safety of his ship.

A crew member went into the aft hold, minutes later emerging with the bad news.

"Captain the hold's flooded; she's got water rushing in through every plank."

The captain and I rushed to the hold and viewed the situation.

"She's gone!" I exclaimed

Looking at each other, the worst was confirmed, the Fox was breaking up, and the tide was rising.

"Won't be long lads, there's boats on the way, look there's another flare." I said pointing in the direction of a white flare which was hanging in the sky a few miles shore side of our position.

I explained to the captain and the crew the position of rescue by the shore boats, as I knew it well, having done many rescues myself. Rigging was cut away from the hull, leaving just the mizzen and fore mast standing, a lamp was hauled up the fore mast and we waited. Nothing else could be done, it was a good job the sea was fairly calm or she'd have gone to pieces within minutes.

It was just past dead low water and the tide was starting to make, not much could happen now; the Fox was hard aground having been almost torn into two pieces, dark was now upon us.

The first of the Deal boats arrived on the scene shortly after dark, a galley with three of my old mates aboard, this boat was to be used to ferry us over to the larger boats which were on their way. Coming alongside the Fox, the boatmen explained what would take place. I kept out of sight on this first encounter, not wanting to be embarrassed by the Deal boatmen on my misfortune of running aground on banks which I for one, ought to know only too well.

The sea was calm and the tide had now risen considerably, there being no immediate danger, in fact the galley stayed alongside us to find out from the crew what had happened and what the cargo was as well. Which they more than likely had more interest in, than actually rescuing us.

Twenty minutes had passed when the light of a larger boat hove too in the deep water about two hundred yards to the nor'east of us. The sea had started to rise much faster and once again the Fox was groaning and cracking, trying to free herself as the swells rocked her deeper into the sand.

"Come on mi hearty's get aboard." Came orders from one of the boatmen in the galley.

Placing a coat on and a large hat on my head, I clambered into the galley with the other crew members un-recognized by the boatmen A short sail took us over to a larger boat, not a Lugger though, one of the cat class boats that were used on the beach, the same type of craft as the Mary-Anne. My worst thoughts were confirmed as we came alongside, of all the luck, it had to be the one boat that I didn't want to be rescued by!

"Get aboard mates, come on now hurry up." Came a familiar stern voice from the stern of the craft. ."Who's the captain, is he amongst you?"

The captain of the Fox addressed his calling while I slid out of sight of the boatman who was skippering the craft, and effectively in charge of the rescue operation.

"I am sir; I'm the captain of the Fox, and I must thank you for your assistance."

"What's her name again captain and what cargo is she carrying?"

"She's called the Fox with a general cargo, not much in her worth salvaging, except a hundred cases or so of whiskey in the fore hold."

"Thanks captain, Whiskey you say! You lads know what to do don't you." He shouted to the crew of the galley eagerly, with a large smile on his face. The skipper of the boat was in his element now, with the knowledge of whiskey aboard, he'd be back out here as fast as his sails to push the old boat.

"I'll get these poor fellows ashore see you later, get as much of that whiskey aboard your galley as you can lads, work quickly now."

The galley disappeared into the darkness back towards the wreck, obviously intent on salvaging as much as they could of the cases of whiskey, while the boat we were in set sail for Deal beach.

"Didn't you have a pilot captain?" asked the skipper of the boat.

"Yes skipper but he wasn't at the helm when she went aground. He was below off watch."

I cowered further under the cover of the other crewmen, trying hopefully not to draw attention to myself.

"Damn fine place to be when running these waters captain, asleep, he shouldn't be allowed to hold a pilots ticket."

"Well my mate was at the helm, he knows the waters, besides we arranged to have Tom taken off when we got to Deal. He's our pilot, he says he lives here, do you know him skipper?"

That's done it I thought, now I'm in for a bashing, once he finds out it's me who was the pilot, I'll never hear the last of it.

The red sea beaten face of the skipper lightened up almost glowing in the dark, nothing made him happier, knowing that he had the last laugh on someone he knew.

"Tom, I wonder, Tom who captain, and you say he hails from Deal!" he exclaimed.

"Don't rightly know his other name skipper, I can't say as if I asked him. He did say he worked with a skipper called Harry, aboard the Mary-Anne of Deal though, do you know him skipper?" asked the captain again.

"The Mary-Anne you say! That's the boat your in now mate and I'm Harry. Well I be a Dutchman's uncle, where is he? Tom! Tom! Come out here lad where are you?"

I pulled myself up from the bilge of the boat; it was no use hiding now, looked at Harry, and then cautiously moved aft, not quite knowing what to expect.

"Tom lad it's good to see you, we heard you foundered on a ship in the North Sea. How are you lad?"

He flung his arms around me, hugging me close glad to see me again, not quite the reaction I was expecting.

"Not bad Harry, I would have been better if someone hadn't dumped me in Ramsgate though." I remarked angrily.

"Oh that! Well we were coming back for you Tom, but you had gone, we was told you took a pilot job on a ship to Lowestoft, we heard, you wasn't coming back to Deal again, that was last we saw of you."

"Yes! Well it's a long story Harry; I'll tell you all about it tomorrow when we're ashore."

I once more settled down on the thwart with the others, waiting until the Mary-Anne made shore.

Some four hours passed before we hove too off Deal pier, it was a pitch dark night and still, a mild night. A signal came from the beach where the Mary-Anne was berthed, all was ready ashore, Harry turned her head shoreward's and with a quiet grating the Mary-Anne gracefully touched the beach.

I along with the rest of the survivors jumped out of the Mary-Anne as soon as she had been hauled clear of the surf and left her crew to haul her up.

We were greeted by a parson and some women at the top of the beach, all of which I knew, and then taken to the local church hall where a hot drink and change of clothes awaited us. Shock took the helpers as they recognized who I was, thus getting me into a long conversation with them, and asking me to tell my adventures as they thought I was dead, drowned in the North Sea. Bidding my shipmates and their captain farewell I left the room and prepared to start making my way home, and to surprise my mother with my good fortune. Harry was standing by the door as I made my way out.

."Good luck mates." I said to the crew of the Fox as I left, then turning and looking Harry in the face, I also bade him goodnight. "I'll see you in the pub in the morning Harry; I think you owe me some wages don't you?"

Harry glared amazed at my comment but he knew what I meant.

The door of our little cottage was unlocked, but looking through the window I could see that there were lights on inside. Knocking quietly I opened the latch and entered the sitting room; mother was sitting in her chair by the fire, knitting by the candle light.

"Hello mother, it's me Tom; I've come home at last." I said in a quiet voice.

She turned and looked at me, not believing her eyes, and then gently raised herself up from the chair.

"Tom, it is, it's my Tom. I thought you were dead, come in lad, shut the door."

Throwing her arms around me she hugged and kissed me, leaving streams of glistening tears rolling down both our faces.

"Aye it's I mother, I've come home at last."

"Tom I can't believe it, sit down lad, I'll make a cup of coco then you can tell me your story. My Tom home at last."

We both sat down by the fire and I told mother what had befell me and how I had fared, explaining in detail what had passed me and what my intentions were. Although pleased to see me, she wasn't too happy about my intentions of going back to Lowestoft.

"Come on Tom, get some sleep, we'll talk again in the morning."

Making our way upstairs we both said our goodnights, and then went into our bedrooms and to sleep. I was woken the following morning at nine with mother shaking me and shouting.

."Get up Tom, get up Tom! There's someone downstairs to see you."

Lazily rolling over on my side and opening my eyes slightly I looked mother in the eyes.

"Who's that mother? Who wants to see me this early in the morning?"

"It's Harry and Dick, they're waiting downstairs for you, come on now, up you get, be smart now."

"Yes, ok, tell them I'll be down in a minute, let me get dressed first."

Climbing out of my bed and dressing, I wondered what Harry and Dick wanted, why had they come to the house so early, and what for?

Downstairs, mother together with Harry and Dick, were sat around the table, a mug of tea steaming in front of each one of them.

"Good morning all. What's with you two, calling here this time of the morning?" I asked as I joined them at the table.

Harry spoke up first, not too sure if he was saying the right things, turning his head with guilt as he tried to get my attention.

"Well Harry, what is it. You haven't come here for a cup of tea now have you?"

An air of quietness fell about the room, and then Harry plucked up enough courage to speak.

"Tom, it's like this, we meant no harm in leaving you in Ramsgate, we were coming back the next day to pick you up but you were gone. You see…."

He went on explaining how it was with himself and Dick, and how they couldn't wake me up the following morning in the inn and thus sailed without me. Then saying sorry for the hurt they had caused to so many, as everyone thought I was dead.

"That's alright Harry, the past is behind us now, the question is, what happened to my share of the catch for that trip eh?"

"I wasn't trying to keep it from you Tom, look here it is. I had it ready from the day you disappeared, I knew you'd be back, here take it."

Harry placed a piece of newspaper in my hand, and then watched as I unrolled it. To my astonishment it contained twenty two pounds, a good sum of money.

"It's all there Tom, we got a good price for the mackerel; I trust that suits you ok?"

."Aye Harry thanks, I knew I could trust you to keep it for me, thanks."

"Now Tom, about your berth. It's still on the Mary-Anne should you want to come back. What'll you say?"

"Sorry Harry I can't, I've commitments in Lowestoft, and I've promised to return there."

Looking at him, and then mother, I went on to tell my story in full of my trip at Lowestoft and what had befallen me. I've one hundred and two pounds now plus my savings, enough to buy a good size house and maybe a boat, so I'm going back to Lowestoft to settle down.

No amount of talking or promises could change my mind. Dick and Harry wished me good fortune and left; Mother, well I tried to get her to come with me but she didn't want to leave Deal.

The next week saw me prepare for my journey back to Lowestoft. I had sorted out all my business, said my farewells boarded the coach and as I thought, had seen Deal for the last time, but this however was not to be so.

****

A good Catch of Sprats

Chapter 11

The Return to Lowestoft

The return trip on the coach to Lowestoft was as uncomfortable as riding the seas around the Goodwin Sands in the Mary-Anne, the weather had turned rough with heavy rain continually falling. The well used roads, if that's what they could be referred to, as they were no more than tracks across fields and through woods, had become sodden, thus causing the wheels of the coach to sink into the soft earth.

As the coach arrived at Lowestoft and pulled up alongside the west quay, I could make out the shape of mother waiting in her long black dress with a shawl hanging over her shoulder, huddled against one of the old wooden fish stores, trying to gain a bit of shelter from the wind. Disembarking and picking up my luggage, I heard a voice from behind calling me.

"Tom! Tom, wait a minute, give me your bags, I'll take those for you."

It was Jimmy; he had been waiting on the other side of the road for me and come running across unseen.

"Welcome back Tom, its good to see you, mother's waiting over there for you."

"Hello Jimmy, good to see you, here take my bag please while I go and say hello to mother."

Making my way to mother I held out my arms and embraced her with every bit of love I had. I hadn't realized how much I could miss someone, but I sure missed her. She kissed me on the cheek; while small droplets of water trickled off her eyelids and fell on my face as the tears of happiness left her pretty eyes.

"Tom my son, how nice to see you again, I didn't believe you were coming back until the letter arrived telling us of your arrival. Come, let's go home and have a warm up and a good meal."

"I'm pleased to be back mother, it's been a hard trip, but I'm glad to see you and Jimmy again." I replied trying to contain the tears that had formed in my eyes.

The three of us proceeded towards the old house, where on entering we were confronted by a hot fire burning in the fire place and the smell of beef stew coming from the kitchen. A welcoming feeling at its best. The evening was spent quietly around the warm log fire, where I told Jimmy and mother what had taken place and about everything that had happened back home in Deal, and that I was now staying in Lowestoft permanently and going to settle down.

The next morning saw us all get back to a normal life, mother busy with her housework and Jimmy and I busy in the harbour getting the Jane-Ellen ready for sea, within half a day I was once again back into the regular routine of fishing. We spent the whole summer bringing in large catches of fish, breaking the port record on two occasions with quantity and weight, working the Jane-Ellen harder than she had ever worked before, not missing one single day's fishing at sea.

I had now managed to save up quite a bit of money again, and during my free time ashore had met a beautiful girl that I had become rather fond of; Mother's approval had been sought and given as well. The young girls name was Judy, a slender but well built lass, with long dark trailing hair and piercing black eyes, the first time I set eyes upon her I just fell in love, strange feeling but it happened. During the next few months we became closer to each other until we both decided that everything being right between us that we would get married, a big decision, but one I never regretted; the date for the wedding was set for early spring.

I worked even harder on the Jane-Ellen with Jimmy for the next six months, taking split shifts to keep the boat at sea and fishing. Jimmy took her on one trip then I took her on the following trip, the money from the catches being pooled and shared out equally between the crews and ourselves. The Jane-Ellen earn't well and broke the port grossing once more just before Christmas by two hundred pounds.

The brief Christmas holiday gave me and Judy a chance to catch up on our lives together, we looked around Lowestoft and the surrounding area for somewhere to live, not too far away as I needed to be as close to the harbour as possible. We found a house in one of the little back streets that ran down behind the Western end of the harbour, a quaint little place with three bedrooms and a nice living room, and kitchen that Judy fell in love with as soon as she saw it; A large black cooking stove graced the entrance of the fireplace, with two built in dressers each side of the chimney breast, lined with shelves where pots and pans could be stored; a pretty little oak table sat in the middle of the floor, surrounded by four equally presentable oak chairs; a white sink with a tap above it was placed conveniently on brick pillars near the back door, it was a kitchen anyone would be proud of. To the rear was a small enclosed garden which would make an ideal vegetable patch should I have the time to tend it, with a long wooden pole situated at each end ,joined by a length of rope; we had our own washing line. We had a good look over the house and discussed it between ourselves; I had saved enough money to buy the house outright and being just right for our needs, I did just that. The house was purchased and cleaned up and a date set for our wedding, March the twentieth.

Another two trips on the Jane-Ellen saw a good grossing again, and then came the day of our wedding, with the boat being laid up for three days and the crew given a holiday.

We were married in the local church with all the bells ringing, a horse and carriage to take us there and a large congregation of people attended; flowers adorned every nook and cranny in the church and were used to decorate the carriage, it was a splendid affair. Judy looked stunning in her white dress with its long trailing silk veil, a day I shall never forget.

We settled down in our house and became not only man and wife but great friends as well, Judy wanted for nothing and I worked hard for her, giving her and the home everything she needed. I being at sea most of the time never had the opportunity to spend much time at home, but after each trip, when I came home, there was always a warm welcome, food on the table and a hug and kiss from Judy that sent quivers through my whole body. A better woman could never have been found. Mother also had become very good friends with Judy, and the two of them spent many hours together, doing what ever women do, when the men are at sea.

A couple of years passed and the Jane–Ellen had been still catching well, with Jimmy and I still working alternate trips to keep her fishing.

It was one October afternoon that Jimmy had taken the Jane-Ellen to sea on a calm still day, not a breath of wind stirred the unbroken surface of the water, uncanny as this surely had to lead to a blow, and it did. The Jane-Ellen had been away for just two days, when one of the fiercest storms ever recorded hit the coast, catching all the boats unawares. The wind freshened up from the nor'west and touched hurricane force, screaming fiercely through the trees and roofs of the houses, the sea had become so rough that the breakers were towering over the harbour wall at a height never seen before, swamping any boats that lie on the wall inside. This day was a day that the port would never forget, as in its fury fourteen boats were lost to the tempest, including the Jane-Ellen

The news of the loss of the Jane-Ellen was bought to us by one of the larger trawlers that landed a day after the wind had decreased, it took both mother and I with shock as there was no sign of survivors, Jimmy and his crew was missing presumed dead, as no one could possibly survive in those conditions. Mother was so distraught that a doctor had to be summoned to give her medication to help her sleep. Poor soul, she was devastated at the loss of Jimmy, he meant everything to her. Judy and I did all we could to make her comfortable, but it was hopeless, for some unknown reason she seemed to have lost the will to live.

The next few days after the storm had abated saw most of the fishing fleet go to sea to look for survivors, with hopes that somewhere a boat might be drifting about, dismasted and helpless. I joined one of the larger sailing drifters on the search. For three days we sailed to and fro on the fishing grounds where most of the missing boats would have been working, an area of around two hundred square miles in size, nothing was found until the last day out, when we picked up the name board of the Jane-Ellen, this confirmed the fears that we had; she was lost and all with her. Arriving back in Lowestoft and being greeted by mother and Judy who were waiting on the quay, I showed them the piece of wreckage that had been found, mother went completely to pieces, I'd never seen a woman cry like that before, it tore her heart out. Two weeks after the loss of the Jane-Ellen mother passed away, breaking the hearts of many souls in the port, as she was so well respected; I don't think she really overcome the loss of poor Jimmy.

Her funeral took place at the local church, with almost all of Lowestoft turning out to pay their respects, a very sad time for all; it's the first time in my life that tears had graced my cheeks for so long and hurt so much. She was laid to rest by her husband in the local church yard, with a beautifully carved headstone being placed on the tomb to mark the place. I missed mother for a very long time and lost all enthusiasm to continue fishing for many months to come.

One quiet summers morning saw Judy and I walking along the harbour wall, looking at the boats below, when on one a notice caught my eye. She was for sale, a beam trawler just like the Jane-Ellen, a smart ship and fully rigged ready to go. I discussed the possibility of buying her with Judy and we agreed that the boat would be ideal for our purpose, and get me back to sea again. I could well afford her as we had sold our little cottage and were living in the big house that mother once lived in and owned. She had in her will left everything to me, something I never expected, so we moved into the big house. The vessel was purchased and once more I started to sail out to the fishing grounds and catch fish, slowly the hurt of losing two people close to me eased off, and once again earnings hit an all time high.

For the next couple of year's life more than exceeded expectation, good money was earn't from my fishing boat, my wife Judy, she supported everything that I did and was a great influence in my life. It was at this period that we considered having a child, after all someone had to carry on in the business after I had either retired or passed away to meet my maker, so between us we decided to start a family.

My wife Judy fell pregnant, which brought great excitement and joy to us both, obviously I was hoping for a boy to carry on my trade During childbirth Judy had unexpected complications well beyond the doctor's capabilities; and something that none of us ever dreamt of happened. Another blow hit me, after four years of marriage, my wife's life ended unexpectedly, Judy died during child birth, nothing could be done to save her or the baby, it devastated me, and it seemed as though my whole world, and everything that I had worked hard to achieve had been destroyed in one evil blow, how could life be so cruel, Judy had so much to live for and was so young; I never really understood the reason for Judy and my child's death, but no doubt the maker in the big house up there in the sky had his reasons.

The weeks passed by , with me just sitting in the house on my own, not knowing what to do, or having the interest to continue working and living in Lowestoft, after all what was the point, I had no one left to care for. After a lot of thought and an agonizing decision, I made my mind up as to what was in reference to my future; I was going to return to Deal, back to the old Mary-Anne and a poorer but happier life plying the Goodwin Sands for a living.

The old house, which had been the start of my career in Lowestoft and held so many happy memories, was put up for sale, and half the money released from it's sale was donated to the Missions to seamen, to help aid other souls that had lost loved ones. My boat was sold and the money along with the remainder on the proceeds from the sale of the house was placed in a secure bank, hopefully for use at a later date, when I might once more, when the time was right, decide to buy my own boat.

My business all sold out in Lowestoft I once again returned to Deal and secured my old berth with Harry in the Mary-Anne; although never forgotten, Lowestoft and the people I loved had played an important part in the laying of my future life, as unbeknown to me a wilder and more daring adventure was to befall me in the very near future, one which would take me far and wide, around to the other side of the world, where I would once again be following my trade and have another beautiful wife beside me. I would in the very near future be leaving Deal forever, on a daring and adventurous trip that even I would have said would not happen, unless fate had shown me a brief look into the future

Deal was to be my home for a very short time after returning, the future of the town had declined, with the modern age of steam causing the demise of the sailing ship, thus rendering most of the boats along the foreshore obsolete as they had no work to do by plying their trade in assisting vessels with stores and supplies. Not many ships became victim to the notorious shippe swallower, the Goodwin Sands, so there was no salvage work. What was to become of me then?

Well that's another story

The End

****

Glossary

Weighed anchor: to lift or raise the anchor or bring the anchor inboard

Bent on: To make fast or to tie on.

Thumper: an extra large swell or sea which normally comes rolling ashore every third swell

Thwart: a seat that fits across the beam of the boat.

Spitting up: to thread herrings onto a long round wooden pole by their gills so they hang down ready to be smoked

Spit: a round pole four feet long and one inch round

Printed in Great Britain
by Amazon